AN EVANS NOVEL OF THE WEST

RED RIVER RUSE

L.J. WASHBURN

M. EVANS & COMPANY, INC. NEW YORK

Library of Congress Cataloging-in-Publication Data

Washburn L. J.

   Red River Ruse / L.J. Washburn.
     p.   cm.—(An Evans novel of the West)
   ISBN 0-87131-653-6 : $16.95
   I. Title.   II. Series.
PS3573.A787R43 1991   91-2384
813'.54—dc20   CIP

M. Evans and Company, Inc.
216 East 49th Street
New York, New York 10017

Manufactured in the United States of America

9 8 7 6 5 4 3 2 1

For Dominick Abel
and Sara Ann Freed

Chapter One

One thing you could say for this part of Texas, Nacho Graves thought as he looked out the window of the swaying, bouncing stagecoach, it had trees. The road was lined with oaks, and the hills that rolled away in the distance were dotted with junipers. Nacho could see where a creek ran with cottonwoods towering along its banks. There was an occasional pecan orchard, too. Most of the trees were losing their leaves now that fall was coming on. The countryside was awash with the browns and golds of the oak leaves as they turned, and the sumacs added their bright red colors.

Yes, Nacho decided, this section of the state was a lot different than where he came from, out in the Pecos River country.

"What are you staring at, Nacho?" Billy Cambridge asked from the seat beside him.

Nacho glanced over at the lawyer. Cambridge wore a dark gray suit that was dusty from traveling, a white shirt and a black string tie, boots and a crisply creased white Stetson. He looked like a respectable, successful attorney, but his eyes still held a hint of those rakehell days when Billy Cambridge had fought Indians and owlhoots to help settle Texas. Shoot, it hadn't even really been that long ago, Nacho thought. Less than a decade had passed since Mackenzie's cavalry had defeated Chief Quanah's forces at the Battle of Palo Duro Canyon and broken the back of Indian resistance on the frontier.

"I was just looking at the trees," Nacho told his traveling companion. "There are not so many like that around Pecos."

Cambridge grinned. "That's the truth. Hell, a five-foot mesquite's a pretty good-sized tree out there."

Nacho turned his attention back to the landscape, leaning slightly out of the window to study the winding trail up ahead. He frowned as he saw several men on horseback suddenly ride into the road from the brush along the side.

"I think we got trouble, Billy," he announced, instinct setting off alarms in his brain. His hand went to the butt of the Colt holstered on his hip.

There were three other passengers in the coach, a married couple sitting opposite Nacho and Cambridge and a drummer on the other side of the lawyer. At the mention of trouble, the salesman reached down and picked up his sample case, holding it tightly to him. The lady clutched her husband's arm and asked apprehensively, "What is it?"

Cambridge held out his hands in a calming gesture. "Don't worry, ma'am," he assured her, although he began to frown as the stagecoach started to slow. "What's going on, Nacho?"

Nacho leaned out the window again. "Riders blocking the road," he said grimly. "Looks like a hold-up."

That brought a gasp from the woman, and her husband's eyes widened. Fear made both of them turn pale. They were well-dressed and looked like Easterners. They had boarded the coach in Fort Worth, and since they hadn't been very sociable, Nacho and Cambridge hadn't found out much about them. The drummer was a typical specimen, portly, middle-aged, nose a little red from too much whiskey over the years. He looked almost as scared as the married couple.

Cambridge reached over and put a hand on Nacho's arm. "Take it easy," he hissed as the coach rocked to a stop. "We don't want a bunch of shooting while there's innocent folks around."

Nacho's jaw tightened angrily, but he jerked his head in a nod and took his hand away from his gun. What Billy said made sense, Nacho supposed, but it was hard to be reasonable when there was twenty thousand dollars at stake.

Maybe the bandits wouldn't find the money. It was in one of the valises stored in the stagecoach's rear boot, put there because Cambridge didn't

2

want to be conspicuous about carrying so much cash. Could be the outlaws would just take the express box and the cash and jewelry the passengers had on them.

Nacho sat tensely on the hard wooden seat as he heard a voice outside say harshly, "Don't try anything, mister. Do like we say and nobody'll get hurt. Now trot them passengers out here."

The stagecoach driver leaned over on the box and called, "Looks like we're bein' held up, folks. Sorry, but you'd best step out of the coach."

Nacho and Cambridge exchanged a quick glance, and then Nacho reached for the door handle. He would be the first one out. He twisted the handle, shoved the door back, and stepped down to the dusty road.

There were six men in the gang, he saw, and they were ranged across the trail so that they completely blocked it. Three of them carried shotguns, which they had trained on the coach and driver. Two of the others were holding revolvers. Only the man who was sitting his horse slightly ahead of the others wasn't holding a weapon of some sort. He was leaning forward in the saddle, his hands crossed casually on his saddle horn. All six of the men wore dusters, hats pulled low, and bandannas tied across the lower half of their faces.

Cambridge got out of the coach, followed by the drummer and the married couple, all three of whom seemed to be having trouble making their muscles work properly. The leader of the gang edged his horse forward, studying the passengers. All that Nacho could see of his face was his eyes, but he could read the danger there.

"Any of you pilgrims try anything, we'll shoot you down," the man said. "Believe it. Now, I want your wallets, your watches, and anything else you got that's worth anything." His eyes swung to Nacho. "Not you, Mex. First thing you do is take that gun out, slow and careful-like, and put it on the ground."

Nacho followed the orders silently, trying to suppress the anger he felt burning inside him. It wasn't surprising that the man had mistaken him for a Mexican. After all, that was half of Nacho's heritage and was plainly visible in his dark eyes, his black hair, and the clothes he wore, especially the short *charro* jacket. He could have just as easily dressed and talked like his British father, but he preferred the *vaquero* outfit.

Billy Cambridge was carrying a gun, too, but it was a short-barreled .38 Colt Lightning, the holster on his left hip concealed under the tail of his coat. Nacho looked at the lawyer again, and Cambridge gave him a tiny shake of the head. They weren't going to start trouble as long as the robbery didn't get out of hand.

The outlaw rode even closer and reached down to pluck wallets from the trembling hands of the drummer and the other man. He looked at the drummer and asked with a sneer in his voice, "What's in the sample case, mister?"

"K-kitchen utensils," the salesman answered. "Everything the modern woman needs to . . . to make her life easier."

"Well, I reckon you can keep them, ace. We ain't got no use for such." The outlaw extended his hand toward the woman. "I'll take that purse, though, lady, and that necklace and your rings."

The woman looked at her husband, but he just licked his lips nervously and didn't say anything. With a sigh, she handed her bag to the robber and then turned over the jewelry.

"You folks are doin' just fine," the man said, and Nacho thought he was grinning under the mask. He came to Billy Cambridge and went on, "You look well-to-do, mister. Hope you got a fat wallet on you."

"Here," Cambridge said flatly, handing over his wallet.

The outlaw took out the roll of bills and riffled through it. "Not bad. What about a watch? You got a watch?"

"I've got one, but I don't intend to turn it over. Sam Houston gave it to me."

"Old Sam himself, eh?" The outlaw pushed back his duster, slid his Colt out of its holster, and thumbed back the hammer as he lined the barrel on Cambridge's face. "Sorry if it's got some sentimental value, mister, but give it over anyway."

Cambridge sighed, pulled the watch from his pocket, and said. "It never kept time worth a damn." He tossed it to the bandit, who plucked it deftly out of the air with his free hand. The barrel of the gun never wavered until it swung over to cover Nacho.

"Now we come to you, Pancho."

"My name is not Pancho. It is Ignacio Alexander Rodriguez Graves."

"I don't give a damn what kind of mongrel you are. I just want your money."

His face flushed, Nacho took out his wallet and gave it to the man.

"All right," the outlaw said, turning his horse toward the driver. "We want the express box, too."

4

"Nothin' in it but mail," the jehu grumbled. He was a wiry old-timer who had been driving stagecoaches for years. In the old days, there would have been a shotgun guard on the seat next to him, but now, with the stagelines dying because of the railroads, the only way to get passengers was to sell tickets as cheaply as possible. That meant cutting corners, which included not paying a salary for a guard.

"Toss it down anyway," the outlaw ordered, and the driver complied. One of the other bandits rode forward, dismounted, and opened the unlocked express box. He dumped the bundles of mail out on the ground with a snort of disgust. The leader of the gang shook his head and went on, "Reckon all that leaves is the baggage in the boot." He nodded to two more of his men. "Go through it."

Nacho had to grit his teeth to keep a groan of dismay from escaping. They were going to find the money and steal it, which meant he was going to be an utter failure in the job he had come along to do. He wished he'd never left the ranch near Pecos. He was a range boss, not a damn bodyguard.

The owner of the spread, Edward Nash, was also an attorney and Billy Cambridge's partner in Pecos's leading law practice. When this business of the money had come up, it had been Nash's idea that his foreman, Nacho Graves, go along with Cambridge to make sure that nothing happened to the money on the way to Fort Smith. Texas might not be the wild and woolly place it had been, but those days weren't long past. The Indian troubles were over for the most part, but there were still plenty of owlhoots roaming the countryside.

Nacho was looking at six of them right now. He hadn't really expected to run into any trouble like this, despite Edward Nash's concern about his partner carrying twenty thousand dollars across the state. But obviously Nash had been right to be worried. He just hadn't picked the right man to accompany Cambridge, Nacho thought bitterly.

The men who had been picked by the leader to check the baggage opened the boot and began going through the valises and trunks inside the compartment. They sprung the locks on each bag in turn and pawed through the contents, tossing them aside to spill heedlessly when they didn't find anything of value.

With each second that passed, they were coming closer to Billy Cambridge's valise, the one containing one thousand twenty dollar bills. The money was on the bottom of the bag, with a stack of clothes on top of it, but Nacho knew better than to hope the outlaws wouldn't discover the bundles of greenbacks.

He looked again at Cambridge, hoping that the attorney would give him some sort of signal. Cambridge's face was stony and expressionless, however.

Nacho sighed. Billy was right. If they grabbed for their guns, they might manage to down one or two of the outlaws—but then they would be riddled by buckshot and .45 slugs. The money would still be gone, and the other passengers and the driver might be wounded or killed, too. As humiliating as it was, they were going to have to swallow this outrage.

"Son of a bitch!"

The exclamation came from one of the bandits going through the baggage, and Nacho didn't have to look in that direction to know the man had just found the money. The other outlaw at the rear of the stage let out a cackle, and the first man ran forward, brandishing one of the bundles. "Look at this!" he called to the leader. "There's a whole pile of money back there!"

The outlaw chief stiffened in his saddle and reached down to snatch the bills away from the other man. He ran his thumb along the edge of the bundle, then turned a dark scowl on the passengers. "Tryin' to hold out on us, were you? Who's this belong to?"

Cambridge took a deep breath. "I'm carrying it, but it's not mine."

"Damn right it's not," the outlaw snapped. "It's ours now."

"I meant that it doesn't belong to me. I'm an attorney, and the money belongs to a client of mine, an old friend. I handled the sale of his ranch for him when he went to live with his daughter in Arkansas, and now I'm delivering the proceeds of the sale to him. I'd surely hate to lose that cash, mister."

The outlaw bounced the money up and down on his palm for a few seconds, then shoved it inside his duster. "Bring me the rest of it," he ordered his men. Within moments, they had brought the other bundles, and the money had been stowed away inside the leader's coat. He turned his angry gaze back to Cambridge and said, "Reckon I can't blame you for hoping we wouldn't find this loot, Mr. Lawyer. But I don't like being held out on, don't like it one damn bit. You took a chance and lost, and now you got to pay."

He was still holding his pistol in one hand, and suddenly, with no more warning than that, he leaned over and slashed at Cambridge's head with the barrel.

"No!" Nacho acted without thinking. Bad enough that he had allowed the money to be stolen. He was not going to stand by and watch his employer's partner and oldest friend be pistol-whipped. Nacho threw himself forward, banging into Cambridge with his shoulder and shoving the attorney out of the way while at the same time grabbing the outlaw's wrist.

"Get him!" the bandit howled as he felt himself being pulled from the saddle by Nacho's unexpected move.

Nacho's fist crashed into the man's face, knocking the mask askew. Before Nacho could get a good look at his face, though, the outlaw threw a punch of his own. The blow caught Nacho on the jaw and sent him staggering back against the stagecoach. He heard the woman passenger screaming and the other outlaws cursing, but there were no gunshots. The gang couldn't risk firing while he was waltzing around with their boss like this.

Keeping his fingers clamped around the outlaw's wrist so that the man couldn't bring the gun to bear on him, Nacho drove a couple of punches into his midsection. The outlaw shrugged them off and brought his knee up toward Nacho's groin. Pinned against the side of the coach the way he was, Nacho couldn't twist completely out of the way. Pain exploded through him as the knee landed.

He doubled over and lowered his head, then butted the outlaw in the face. Might as well try to turn the pain to his advantage. That thought flashed through his mind. He tried to loop a punch to his opponent's head, but the man blocked it.

A solid left cross jerked Nacho's head to the side. He heard more yelling, caught a glimpse of Billy Cambridge struggling in the grasp of the two outlaws who had found the money. The other three bandits were still covering the rest of the party. Suddenly, a gun butt came down on Cambridge's head, and he sagged in the grip of the men he was fighting.

Nacho cried, "Billy!" when he saw that happen, but he didn't have time for any other reaction. The gang leader hit him again and tore his arm free from Nacho's weakening grasp. Nacho spotted his Colt on the ground several feet away. The only option he had left was a desperate dive for the gun—

He heard the roar of exploding gunpowder, felt something burn across his side like a white-hot poker. Twisting from the impact of the shot, he pitched to the ground. His fingers fell short of the butt of his gun by a good foot, and he couldn't seem to make them move any closer, no matter how badly he wanted to pick up the revolver and blow that smirk off the face of the man who had just shot him. Nacho still couldn't see all of his features, but the bandanna had gotten twisted aside enough to reveal the arrogant grin on the man's lips.

That was the last thing Nacho saw for a while.

Billy Cambridge struggled back to consciousness first, although he didn't know it at the time. All he knew was that his head hurt like blazes and that he was stretched out on the ground with the taste of dirt in his mouth.

He lifted his head, groaned, and spat out as much of the grit as he could. The effort made his skull ring like an anvil, but the pain told him he was still alive and he was grateful for that much. His memory was fairly clear. He remembered the fight with the outlaws and he knew that once it had started, he could have easily gotten killed in the fracas—

Nacho. Where was Nacho?

Cambridge blinked his eyes open, got his hands under him, and rolled over. He saw sky and trees and then a worried face with three days' growth of beard peering down at him.

"You all right, mister?" the stagecoach driver asked anxiously.

Cambridge lifted his arm. "Give me a hand," he managed to say. "I've got to sit up."

The jehu grasped Cambridge's wrist and hauled him upright. A fresh series of hammerblows landed inside the lawyer's head for a few seconds, then gradually subsided. He looked around and saw the drummer and the married couple standing beside the coach, all three of them looking pale and shaken. Cambridge turned his head, searching for Nacho, fear growing inside him.

The ranch foreman was stretched out on the ground several yards away. His jacket was open, and Cambridge saw the splash of red on his white shirt, the blood standing out in awful contrast.

"Oh, hell," Cambridge whispered. Nacho Graves was a good man, one of the best hands to ever ride the West Texas range, but more than that, Cambridge considered him a friend. Quite a few years separated the two men, but that didn't matter. Cambridge had an appreciation for fine old

8

whiskey and high stakes poker, while Nacho was more interested in the señoritas. And that wasn't important, either.

Cambridge stood up and staggered over to Nacho, ignoring the assistance the driver tried to give him. Kneeling next to the younger man, Cambridge put a couple of fingers on Nacho's throat and searched for a pulse. Within a few seconds, he had located a strong, regular beat, and a great sigh of relief came from the lawyer. He looked up at the driver and asked, "What happened?"

"After those hombres knocked you out, the one who was leadin' 'em got loose from your friend here and took a shot at him. He went right down—your friend, I mean—and for a second I thought that fella was going to empty all six into him. But then he yelled for the others to cut the leaders and mount up, and he got on his own horse and they rode out of here. Hollered back for nobody to come after 'em. Said they'd kill anybody that did."

Cambridge glanced at the coach. Sure enough, the lead horses were gone, driven off by the outlaws as they rode away. The coach had been using a four-hourse hitch, another money-saving measure, and that meant there were only two horses left to pull the vehicle on to the next stop.

"How far are we from the Red River station?" Cambridge asked.

The driver spat on the road. "A good ten miles, I reckon. It'll take us quite a spell to get there, the shape we're in."

Cambridge nodded in agreement and said, "Help me with this man. I want to take a look at that bullet wound now. It might not wait until we get to the station."

With the driver's help, Cambridge got Nacho propped up and the jacket and shirt stripped away from the wound. It was messy, sure enough, but Cambridge hoped the crease was a shallow one. He turned to the drummer and said, "Give me the flask you've got in your pocket."

"F-flask?" the man hedged. "I don't recall saying I was carrying a flask—"

"Damn it, give me the whiskey." Cambridge's voice was sharp. Moderating his tone, he turned his attention to the woman and went on, "And if you've got a handkerchief, ma'am, I could use it."

"Of course," she said, taking a soft cloth from a pocket of her dress.

"I'm afraid it won't be much good for anything once I get through with it," Cambridge apologized as he took the handkerchief from the woman.

"That's all right." She cast a glance at her husband, not an angry look but perhaps a disappointed one. "You and your friend had the courage to stand up to those highwaymen. I'm glad to help now."

Cambridge didn't tell her that he would have preferred not to get into a fight with the outlaws. He cast a cold-eyed glance toward the drummer and said, "What about that whiskey?"

The salesman sighed, pulled a silver flask from his hip pocket, and handed it over.

Cambridge poured a little of the liquor on the cloth and began cleaning away the blood from Nacho's injured side. Nacho let out a moan and shifted slightly from the pain, but he didn't regain consciousness. As the blood was washed off, Cambridge was relieved to see that the crease was indeed a shallow one, little more than a bullet burn. He'd finish cleaning it up, maybe get some strips of the lady's petticoat to use for bandages, and Nacho would be fine once he'd had some rest and recovered the strength that had leaked out of him along with the blood. Cambridge had patched up dozens of wounds that were worse, sometimes with bullets or arrows or both whizzing over his head.

By the time Cambridge was finished, Nacho was moaning again and his eyelids were fluttering. When his eyes finally opened and stayed that way, he stared up at Cambridge and said weakly, "Billy? You are all right?"

"I'm fine," Cambridge grunted. "I'll have a headache for a while, but at least I'm better off than you. You ruined a perfectly good shirt, amigo. Got blood all over it."

"I remember now. I am shot, no?"

"You are shot, yes." Cambridge slipped an arm around Nacho's shoulders and gently, carefully, lifted him into a sitting position. "But it's just a scratch. You'll be all right."

"I'm not dying?"

"Not hardly."

Nacho shook his head. "I was hoping I was mortally wounded."

"Why the devil would you hope that?" Cambridge exclaimed.

"Those bandits . . . They got the money, didn't they?"

"They got the money," Cambridge admitted. "But that's not your fault, Nacho."

"Yes, it is. Mr. Nash told me to be sure that nothing happened to you or that money. And I let a bunch of second-rate desperados hit you on the head and take the cash and did nothing to stop them—"

The words were coming faster out of Nacho now. Cambridge grimaced and said quickly, "I told you not to blame yourself. I should have hidden it better. If anybody has to take the blame, it's me."

For a long moment, Nacho frowned at him in thought, then said, "Billy, if it's anybody's fault, it's that skunk who took the money. What say we go find him?"

Cambridge had to grin. "I was starting to think the same thing myself."

The driver sidled up to them and said, "If you fellas are up to travelin' now, we'd best get movin'. Be after dark as it is before we get to the Red. You never know, there might be more owlhoots along this trail."

The man was right. Cambridge said to him, "Take Nacho's other arm and let's get him on his feet."

After a moment's dizziness, Nacho seemed to be fairly stable. He looked a little gruesome in his blood-stained clothes, but a healthy slug of what was left in the drummer's flask began to put some color back in his face. He was able to pick up his flat-crowned black hat and settle it on his head. Frowning, he looked around. "Where's my gun?" he asked.

"Outlaws took it," the driver said. "Got my six-gun and greener, too."

Nacho sighed, and Cambridge knew he regretted the loss of the pistol. "Then I guess I'm ready when the rest of you folks are. . . ." the foreman said.

Cambridge picked up his own Stetson, pushed its dented crown back into shape, and placed it carefully on his graying hair, avoiding the tender lump where the gun butt had landed. The married couple was already back on board the stage. The drummer climbed in next, followed by Nacho and Cambridge. With only two horses to pull the load, the coach lurched even more than usual as it began to roll along the road toward the Red River station. Cambridge didn't care.

Comfort didn't matter anymore, he thought grimly. What was important was getting that money back—and getting his hands on the men who had stolen it.

Chapter Two

The pain in Nacho's side had settled down to a dull ache, and Cambridge had wrapped the bandages around him so tightly that he was having a little trouble breathing. Every jolt of the stagecoach sent a twinge of pain through his head. Other than that, he thought, he didn't feel too bad for somebody who'd been shot by a no-good outlaw.

When his mind had started working coherently again after regaining consciousness, his first thoughts had been of going after the bandits and recovering the stolen money. He was glad to discover that Cambridge's thinking was running along the same lines. Anger burned inside Nacho, deeper than the pain from the bullet wound.

"Did you ever get a good look at the leader's face while you were tangling with him?" Cambridge asked.

Nacho shook his head. "I got the impression he was an ugly son-of-a-buck, but that's all."

"Well, he could have killed all of us. I guess we're lucky to be alive."

Luck had nothing to do with it, Nacho thought. Fate had decreed that they survive the encounter with the outlaws, so that they could hunt down the lawless dogs and avenge themselves. He kept himself insulated from the pain with that thought.

He'd been a little uneasy about this trip ever since he and Billy Cambridge had left Pecos. Established as a railroad stop, Pecos was right on the Missouri Pacific and it would have been simple to take a train from there to Fort Worth and then on to Fort Smith to deliver the money. But Cambridge had gotten it into his head that he wanted to go on the stagecoach. "With the way the railroads are expanding, it won't be much longer until the stage lines are all gone," Billy had said. "Besides, it might even be safer. There have been a lot of train robberies lately." Nacho had to admit he was right about that. And it was still possible to travel from West Texas to Arkansas by stage, although you had to change from one small, struggling line to another half a dozen times.

Then there was the matter of the cash. It would have been simpler and safer to send a bank draft, but old Simon Prescott had insisted on cash, and he had insisted that his friend Billy Cambridge bring it to him. They had fought together in the Cortinas War a quarter of a century earlier under the command of Captain Rip Ford, Cambridge as a young man, Prescott already a middle-aged, veteran Ranger at the time. According to Cambridge, Prescott had saved his life a time or two during that bloody border skirmish, and whatever Prescott wanted now, Cambridge was going to do his best to deliver.

The situation had worried Edward Nash, too, and since he was involved in a complicated legal case back in Pecos and couldn't leave at the moment to accompany Cambridge, Nacho had been more than willing to take his place. He and Billy Cambridge had always gotten along well, Cambridge treating him as an equal rather than as a hired hand, and a part-Mexican one at that.

"We'll have to report this outrage to the authorities," the man sitting across from Nacho and Cambridge was saying. "Maybe they can track down those criminals."

The drummer snorted in contempt. "Don't bet on it, friend. I've been through these parts before, and the law around here isn't going to care about some piddling stage holdup. The sheriff'll have other things on his mind—like the next election."

"The robbery has to be reported anyway," Cambridge put in. "That's the thing to do."

"But if the law won't do anything"—the woman spoke up—"what's the use?"

"I'm an attorney, ma'am," Cambridge told her. "It's always best to follow the proper channels, even when the purpose of it isn't readily apparent."

14

Nacho wasn't so sure about that. Seemed to him that the best way to deal with this problem would be to find those owlhoots and take the money back, at gunpoint if necessary, and proper channels be damned. If Billy wanted to talk to the authorities first, though, Nacho supposed it wouldn't do any harm.

As the driver had predicted, night had fallen before the stagecoach reached the Red River. Actually, the river marking the border between Texas and the Indian Territory was still about an eighth of a mile ahead when the coach pulled up in front of a sturdy building made of wide, thick planks. A lantern hung from the ceiling over a porch along the front of the building. Out back was a large barn where spare teams for the coaches were kept.

Another building much like the first one sat about twenty yards away. Its porch was lit by a lantern, too, and its large double doors were open. This building looked to be more neatly kept than its companion, and a sign over the door proclaimed it to be the Red River Trading Post and Mercantile, Theodore Maxwell, Esq., Prop.

As the passengers climbed out of the coach, Cambridge looked over at the trading post sign and frowned. "Theodore Maxwell," he read. "Must be Jake's boy. I hope nothing's happened to Jake. It's been ten years or more since I've seen him."

The words were barely out of Cambridge's mouth when the door of the first building opened and a tall, slender man stepped out, a worried look on his weathered face. "What happened, Rufus?" he called out to the driver. "You're runnin' late."

"We had some trouble, Jake," the driver replied. "Some gents held us up."

"I see now the leaders are gone," Jake Maxwell said as he came closer. "Anybody hurt?"

The driver gestured toward Nacho and Cambridge. "These two gentlemen got roughed up, and the fella who was leadin' the gang shot one of 'em."

Maxwell swore emphatically. As he stepped up to the passengers and saw their faces, he let out another exclamation. "Billy Cambridge!" he said. "What are you doin' in this neck of the woods?"

"Well, I didn't come to look at your ugly face, you old hoss." Cambridge clapped Maxwell on the shoulder. "But I reckon it is good to see you again, Jake." The attorney turned to Nacho. "My friend here caught a bullet during that robbery. He could use some hot food and a little rest."

"Not as much as I could use a chance to even the score with the man who did this," Nacho said.

Cambridge performed the introductions. "Nacho, this is an old friend of mine, Jake Maxwell. Jake, meet Nacho Graves."

The two men shook hands, their work-roughened palms gripping firmly, and Maxwell said, "Glad to meet you, Nacho."

"Ignacio Alexander Rodriguez Graves," Nacho supplied with a grin. "But any old friend of Billy's can call me Nacho, Mr. Maxwell."

"Come on inside, son. Billy patch up that wound of yours?"

Nacho nodded.

"I'm sure he did a good job, but like he said, you could still use some hot grub. I been keepin' the stew warm 'till the stage got here. All of you folks come in and rest a spell."

Nacho felt an instinctive liking for Jake Maxwell. The leathery stationkeeper was a few years older than Cambridge, but he moved like a much younger man and there were only a few streaks of silver in his thick black hair. Nobody could call Maxwell a particularly handsome man although he had a certain dignity about him.

The married couple babbled to Maxwell about the holdup as everyone went into the station. Inside, the building was furnished simply and functionally, with a long table flanked by benches dominating the big main room. A large, wood-burning, cast iron stove sat in one corner, and there was a fireplace in another corner. A couple of armchairs were pulled up in front of the fireplace, which was not lit on this mild autumn night. In a few weeks, as fall settled in over North Texas, a fire would feel good against the evening chill.

As Nacho caught a whiff of what was simmering in the big pot on the stove, he drew in as deep a breath as he could with the bandages strapped around him and grinned. He was hungrier than he had realized. He guessed losing so much blood was responsible for that. At the moment, he felt just about as wobbly-legged as a newborn calf, and it would be good to sit down and put away some food.

Maxwell ladled out bowls of the savory stew and poured cups of coffee for the hungry passengers and driver, then said, "While you folks are eating, I'll see about changing the team."

"Need a hand, Jake?" Cambridge asked. "I didn't notice any hostlers around."

16

Maxwell shook his head. "No, thanks, I been changin' teams by myself for so long, I've got it down to an art, Billy." With a grin and a wave, he went out.

Cambridge turned to Nacho, who was already wolfing down his bowl of stew. "Better take it easy there. Your system's already had one shock today. You don't want to give it another one."

"You said I needed to eat, Billy," Nacho replied. "And you know how I like to eat."

That was true enough. Nacho's skill with a knife and fork was legendary around the bunkhouse and in the whole Pecos area, in fact. Hard work kept him from gaining weight, however.

"You're not chasing cows ten hours a day now," Cambridge pointed out. "Anyway, when you get through, we'll go through your gear and find you some clean clothes."

Nacho nodded and went back to the stew. He was just a growing boy with a healthy appetite, he told himself. Besides, he had to recuperate from the bullet wound, and that would take plenty of nourishment.

"Where can we find the sheriff around here?" the husband asked. "I still intend to report that robbery."

"You'd have to go clear back down to Sherman," the drummer replied. "I tell you, it's not worth it. I lost my money, too, you know, but I'm just going to wire my home office to send me an advance."

"I suppose I could wire my bank in St. Louis for traveling expenses," the man mused. "Our tickets are already paid for until we can get back home."

Cambridge said, "We can probably find a deputy or a constable around here who could take our report of the holdup. I'm sure Mr. Maxwell, the stationkeeper, can tell us where to find someone in authority.

Before the discussion could continue, a footstep in the doorway made everyone at the table look up. They were all still a little jumpy, Nacho supposed.

But even though he had tensed at the sound of someone entering, he relaxed immediately when he saw who it was. A grin broke out on his face. That was an instinctive reaction on the part of Nacho Graves whenever a pretty girl came into a room.

This girl was pretty, no doubt about that. She had thick blond hair that fell in long, shining waves past her shoulders. Her eyes were a brilliant blue, even in the fairly dim lanternlight of the stage station. The creamy skin of her forehead creased in a frown as she looked around the room and said, "Oh, excuse me. I was looking for Jake."

Billy Cambridge stood up politely, and Nacho was only a second behind him, not wanting to be outdone in manners by his companion, not where a lovely creature like this was concerned. Cambridge introduced himself and Nacho and then said, "Jake went to hitch a fresh team to the stagecoach. Didn't you see him outside?"

The girl shook her head. "No, he must have been out in the barn. I'll go find him."

"If there is anything we can do for you . . .?" Nacho spoke up.

She smiled, and Nacho forgot about the pain in his side and the ache in his head. "No, that's all right," the girl said. "I'll find Jake."

She turned and went out, and Nacho and Cambridge took their seats again. The salesman leaned forward, the smile on his florid face threatening to turn into a leer, and said, "Mighty pretty girl. You reckon she works here?"

"I don't know," Cambridge replied. "But if she comes back in, I hope everyone will be polite to her. Any lady deserves that much respect." He looked meaningfully at the drummer.

"Sure, sure," the man said hurriedly. "I didn't mean anything, mister. Just commenting on the young lady's attractiveness."

"You got to admit she was mighty pretty, Billy," Nacho added.

"Don't you start," Cambridge told him. "Every time you see a pretty girl . . ." He broke off with a shake of his head.

A few minutes later, the door opened again and Jake Maxwell came in. "I'll have that team hitched up in a few minutes," he said, "but you folks just take your time with that meal. I know you've been through a lot today."

"We already lost quite a bit of time on the schedule, Jake," the driver said. "Got to make it up."

Maxwell waved off that objection. "No need bustin' a gut doin' it." He turned back toward the door.

Before he could leave, Cambridge stopped him by saying, "There was a young woman in here a minute ago looking for you, Jake. She find you?"

Maxwell nodded. "Yeah, she came back to the barn. That's my daughter-in-law, Sandra. Married to Ted—Theodore, he calls himself now. Don't know if you recollect him or not, Billy."

"He was just a sprout last time I saw him," Cambridge grinned.

"I gave him the tradin' post as a weddin' present when him and Sandy got hitched. Keepin' up with both places was gettin' to be too much for an old-timer like me, anyway. This station's enough to keep me busy now."

Maxwell went out of the room quickly without saying anything else or giving Cambridge a chance to prolong the conversation. Nacho had only glanced up from his bowl a couple of times while the two men were talking, but he had a feeling Jake Maxwell was uncomfortable discussing his daughter-in-law. Maxwell hadn't seemed to want to meet Billy's eyes, and he'd left abruptly, like he was afraid of saying too much. From the frown on Cambridge's face, Nacho thought Maxwell's behavior must have struck his friend as a little strange, too.

Nobody else had noticed anything unusual, though. The others were still eating hungrily. Thinking that maybe he had been mistaken, Nacho turned his attention back to the stew.

When Maxwell reappeared, he announced, "Coach is ready to go."

"Where's the nearest telegraph office?" the drummer asked. "I've got to wire my office."

"And I need to send a message to my bank," the other man added.

"That'd be across the river in Indian Territory. There's a Western Union office in Durant, and you'll be goin' through there tomorrow." Maxwell poured himself a cup of coffee, then came over to the table and straddled one of the benches near Cambridge. "It's a shame we didn't get to visit longer, Billy. But I reckon you've got business and have to be movin' on."

"Not so fast," Cambridge said grimly. "I've got business to take care of, all right, but it's right here. I want to report that holdup to the law, Jake. I figure you can tell me where to find the nearest constable or deputy sheriff."

Maxwell frowned. "There's a deputy from the sheriff's office down in Sherman that rides up this way every few days, but telling him about the robbery ain't goin' to do much good. Those owlhoots are long gone, Billy."

"They could come back," Cambridge said. "Maybe after today, they'll decide the pickings are good in this part of the country."

Maxwell looked down at his coffee cup. After a moment's silence, he finally said, "Well, to tell you the truth, this ain't the first time that bunch has hit around here. They've held up stages and robbed stores and generally made life miserable for folks. So you see, the sheriff already knows they're operatin' around here. He don't stand a chance in hell of catchin' 'em, though. He's more politician than manhunter." Maxwell shook his head. "It ain't like the old days when we were ridin' with Rip Ford, Billy."

"I know that," Cambridge said with a sigh. "Nacho suggested we go after the bandits ourselves. From what you're saying, it's starting to sound like he was right."

Maxwell's head jerked up, genuine alarm etched on his features. "You're goin' to try to track down those outlaws?" he demanded.

"I'm thinking about it. They stole a sizable amount of money that belongs to one of my clients, and I can't conclude my business until I recover it."

The stagecoach driver leaned forward to join the conversation. "Does that mean you two gents won't be goin' on with the rest of us?"

"That's exactly what it means," Cambridge replied solemnly. He looked back at Maxwell and went on, "I'm hoping that you can put us up for a while, Jake."

"Sure, sure, that ain't a problem." Something was obviously bothering Maxwell, though. He hesitated, then said, "Are you sure you ain't gettin' a mite . . . old to be chasin' outlaws, Billy?"

Nacho grinned slightly and waited for the explosion. It didn't come. Cambridge just said quietly, "I'm not as young as I used to be, but none of us are. I can still ride a horse and handle a six-gun, and Nacho here has been tracking since he was a boy. I think between us we'll at least have a chance of locating that gang. When we do, we'll lead the authorities to their hide-out. I haven't totally lost my senses, Jake. I'm not going up against half a dozen hardcases unless I have to."

"You always were a stubborn old cuss, even when you were a youngster," Maxwell said with a grimace. But then a grin spread over his face. "All right, you're welcome to stay, both of you. And I'll do what I can to help out."

"Thanks, Jake."

The driver stood up and motioned for the remaining passengers to follow him. "We got to get rollin'," he said. To Cambridge, he added, "Good luck, mister. I got a feelin' you're goin' to need it."

Within moments, the stagecoach was on its way, minus the gear belonging to Nacho and Cambridge. If it had been possible, the Red River crossing should have been made before dark, but there was a good ford with a solid bottom, and the river was shallow at this time of year. The driver knew the route quite well, too. The coach would be able to make the crossing without any trouble and push on into the Indian Territory.

Maxwell helped his two visitors carry their baggage into the station.

building, saying, "I warn you, the accommodations ain't goin' to be fancy. But since there ain't nobody else stayin' here right now, at least you can each have a room to yourself. The grub's good, that much I can promise you."

"I may never leave," Nacho said with a grin.

Despite the front he was putting up, he was getting tired. Suffering a gunshot wound, even a minor one, took a lot out of a man. He was looking forward to a good night's rest. No matter how lumpy the bunk was, it wouldn't keep him from sleeping.

Several narrow doors opened off the main room of the station, leading into cubicles where passengers could spend the night if the stagecoach could not go on until morning. Maxwell pointed to the door on the left and said, "I bunk in there, if you need anything. You boys can take your pick of the other rooms."

"These'll do fine," Cambridge said, indicating two doors in the middle of the row. He opened one of the doors and peered into the room, then carried his bags inside. Maxwell followed him.

Nacho was about to go into the other room when he heard the building's front door open behind him. He glanced over his shoulder, then turned around quickly when he saw Sandra Maxwell entering the main room. She closed the door behind her and turned around, stopping short as she saw Nacho standing there.

"Hello," she said after a second. "I thought the stagecoach had gone on."

He realized he was wearing his hat and snatched it off. "It has. But my friend and I, we stayed behind."

"You've been hurt!" Sandra exclaimed, suddenly stepping closer. "There's blood all over your shirt."

Nacho grinned. "It looks a lot worse than it really is. It's just a bullet crease. Some men held up the stage."

"Yes, Jake told me about it. But he didn't say that anyone would be staying behind. Are you hurt too badly to travel?"

"Oh, no," Nacho said with a shake of his head. "I'm fine, really. My amigo and I just have some business to take care of before we go on to Fort Smith." He wasn't sure how many details of the situation he wanted to give her, but he realized there was no need to be suspicious of her. Maxwell would probably tell her all about it, anyway. Quickly, he sketched in the problem he and Cambridge were facing concerning the stolen money.

Sandra drew nearer while he was talking, and Nacho suddenly scowled as he noticed the dark, swollen spot on her jaw. When he had first seen her, she was inside the doorway of the building, and the light hadn't been good enough for him to spot the bruise. Now he had no trouble seeing it.

As if she sensed what he was looking at, Sandra lowered her head and turned away slightly. "I'm sorry you were hurt," she said softly. "If there's anything I can do to help . . ."

"I just need some sleep," he told her. "I'm getting pretty tired."

"Of course. Well, I'm sure I'll be seeing you again if you're staying around these parts for a while. Good night, Mr. Graves."

"Wait a minute," he said quickly. "Weren't you looking for your father-in-law?"

"I can talk to Jake another time. It was nothing important. Good night."

Before he could stop her again, she was out the door. Nacho frowned at the spot where she had disappeared. He had always considered himself pretty level-headed and certainly not given to imagining things. But he sensed somehow that something was wrong here at the Red River station. Jake Maxwell had seemed surprised and not very enthusiastic about their decision to stay for a while, at least at first, and there was the matter of the bruise on Sandra Maxwell's face. Nacho wondered how it had gotten there.

None of his business, he told himself. He had to worry about helping Cambridge recover that twenty thousand dollars, or as much as possible of it. If it took them very long to catch up to the outlaws, all the money might already be spent.

Cambridge and Maxwell came out of the room where they had gone a few minutes earlier. They were chuckling, and Nacho figured they had been talking about old times. Cambridge's features became more serious as he looked at Nacho and said, "You'd better turn in. You're looking a little pale again."

Nacho nodded. "I will. Your daughter-in-law came in looking for you again, Mr. Maxwell." Sandra hadn't asked him to pass along that message, but Nacho didn't see what it could hurt.

Maxwell nodded curtly, a strange veiled look dropping down over his eyes. "I'll mosey over to the tradin' post and see what she wants," he said. "'Night, Billy."

"Good night, Jake." When Maxwell was gone, Cambridge said to

Nacho, "You want me to take those bandages off and have a look at that wound again?"

"It'll keep 'til morning," Nacho told him. "Right now I just want to rest."

"That's the best idea. Good night."

The bunk was lumpy, all right, Nacho discovered a few minutes later when he stretched out on it. But that didn't keep him from sleeping. It was something else that kept him staring up at the darkened ceiling for long minutes that turned into an hour or more.

But damned if Nacho could have said what that something was.

Chapter Three

Nacho finally fell asleep, and when he did, he slept soundly. So soundly that he did not awaken until the sun was already a considerable distance above the horizon the next morning and shining brightly through the single small window in the little room.

The wound and the muscles around it had stiffened up during the night, he discovered as he tried to nimbly swing his feet off the bunk and stand up. Biting back a gasp of pain, he made a second attempt, more slowly this time. He was able to get to his feet, but he was still hunched to one side against the pain. Straightening took another effort, as did pulling on his pants and a clean shirt. Finally, though, he was dressed, and he opened the door and stepped carefully into the main room of the station. The scent of coffee and bacon drew him on and gave him strength.

There was no one in the room, but the coffee pot was on the stove, as was a pan of biscuits and bacon. Nacho helped himself, standing up at the stove to eat rather than sitting at the table. Getting up and down was too hard at the moment. He was confident that he would loosen up some as the day went along. He already felt better, the food working quickly to replenish his strength.

A few minutes later, Billy Cambridge and Jake Maxwell came in, and Nacho raised an eyebrow in surprise when he saw how the lawyer was dressed. Cambridge wore the same Stetson he had been sporting the day before, but the suit had been replaced by denim pants, a light blue work shirt, and a bandanna knotted around Cambridge's throat. A shell belt was fastened around his waist, and in the holster it supported was a blued steel, walnut-butted Colt revolver.

"Billy!" Nacho exclaimed. "You look like one of the ranch hands!"

"I was riding the range before you were born, amigo," Cambridge told him. "Jake loaned me the shirt and the gun. The way I see it, I won't be doing much lawyering for a while. I'll put the suit back on when there's a use for it."

Nacho grinned. "If *Señor* Nash could see you now, he would be surprised."

"He'd probably put me to work in the round-up," Cambridge grunted. "How are you feeling this morning?"

"Like a stampede ran over me. But I'll be all right."

"You won't be able to ride for a day or two," Cambridge said. "While you're mending a little, I'll hunt up that deputy Jake mentioned and tell him about the robbery. You stay around here and rest."

A grimace pulled at Nacho's mouth, but he nodded. "I reckon that'd be best. But Billy . . . don't do anything foolish." He grinned again. "At least not until I'm along and can have some fun, too."

"Sure." Cambridge turned to Maxwell and went on, "I hate to bother you for anything else, Jake, but if I could have the loan of a good saddle horse . . ."

"I've got one you can use," Maxwell said, putting a hand on Cambridge's shoulder as both of them went out.

Nacho sighed. He didn't like being left behind, and he liked the idea of Billy Cambridge riding around this rugged countryside by himself even less. There was no telling what Billy might run into. But Nacho knew if he got on a horse today, the wound in his side would tear open and he'd be worse off than when he started. He would just have to hope that Cambridge could stay out of trouble for a day or two.

He poured himself another cup of coffee and picked up another biscuit. If he was going to be stuck here, he might as well enjoy it, he thought.

Billy Cambridge had a lot on his mind as he rode the borrowed saddle horse back along the trail that the stagecoach had covered the day before. He planned to find the spot where the robbery had taken place and see if there were any tracks left to indicate where the bandits might have been headed. When he had done that, he would ride over to the Sand Ridge Baptist Church, about three miles east of the Red River stage station. According to Jake Maxwell, the ladies of the church's congregation provided lunch on the grounds every Wednesday at noon. This was Wednesday, and also according to Maxwell, the church was the most likely spot to find Bart Gilliam, the sheriff's deputy from the county seat at Sherman.

Cambridge was thinking about other things besides the hold-up and the stolen twenty thousand dollars, though. Jake Maxwell had been cordial enough since the travelers arrived at the station, but the lawyer sensed that something was bothering his old friend. Maxwell had always been an open sort, the type to put all his cards on the table. Now Cambridge had an idea Maxwell was keeping something bothersome to himself, keeping his worries bottled up inside. That would take a toll on an outgoing sort like Jake, Cambridge thought.

He pushed those speculations aside for the moment as he reached a familiar stretch of road. Seeing the clump of trees and brush where the outlaws had hidden until they rode out to stop the stage, Cambridge reined in and studied the layout.

From the looks of things, there hadn't been much traffic along here since the previous afternoon. He could see the ruts in the dust that had been laid down by the iron wheels of the stage and the muddled mass of tracks left by the horses while they were stopped and nervously shifting around. Carefully, Cambridge walked his own mount around the scene. He picked out the tracks that had most likely been made by the outlaws' horses. The trail led off from the road at an angle to the southwest, and that jibed with what the driver and the other passengers had told Cambridge after the robbery.

He leaned forward in his saddle and studied the terrain spread out before him. That was rugged country over there, he knew, full of gullies and creeks and rocky hills. There would be hiding places a-plenty for someone who knew the country, and Cambridge had a feeling those outlaws were quite familiar with it. Tracking them down wouldn't be easy.

He and Nacho were going to do exactly that, though, unless the authorities could hold out some hope of catching the bandits. And from what Maxwell had said, Cambridge doubted that would happen.

The attorney started to swing his horse around. He could cut across country from here to reach the church. It had been a while since he had passed through these parts, but he was confident he could still find his way. Suddenly, Cambridge stiffened in the saddle, instinct warning him that someone was watching him. His eyes searched the surrounding countryside, looking for some sign of whoever might be spying on him.

Was this an ambush? Somehow, he didn't think so. His muscles weren't braced for the impact of a bullet. But he didn't want to take a chance. Quickly, he heeled the horse into the stand of trees at the side of the road, his hand going to the butt of the borrowed revolver at the same time.

The sound of hoofbeats came to Cambridge's ears. He twisted in the saddle, trying to locate them. They were off to his left, he thought, and heading east. Whoever it had been was in a hurry now. Cambridge rode out of the brush and looked in the direction of the rapidly fading sounds, but he was unable to spot any movement. There were too many trees between him and the rider.

Cambridge frowned. There was no way of knowing for sure that someone had been spying on him. The rider could have been just another traveler in a hurry.

But Cambridge's hunches had helped keep him alive for a long time, and his belly was telling him now that somebody was taking an unhealthy interest in him.

He kept an eye on his back trail, and instead of heading across country, as he had intended to earlier, he followed the road nearly all the way back to the stage station before he turned onto an eastbound cut-off that would take him to the church. A check of his watch told him it was almost noon.

There were quite a few buggies and wagons parked in front of the church when he arrived, along with several saddle horses. Tables were set up under the trees next to the steepled building of whitewashed clapboard, and ladies in sun bonnets and calico dresses bustled around. Platters of fried chicken, ham, and pot roast were set out on the tables, along with potato salad, black-eyed peas, beans, sweet potatoes, and greens. One table was loaded down with cakes and pies. Cambridge grinned as he looked over the spread. Nacho would be sorry he had missed this meal, but Cambridge hoped to have wrapped up his business in this part of the country and be gone by the next Wednesday.

Quite a few cowboys were on hand, punchers from the nearby ranches, Cambridge guessed. In exchange for listening to a short sermon from the church's pastor, the waddies would get to partake of food cooked and served by ladies, rather than by some bald-headed, grizzle-bearded, tobacco-chewing ranch cook. From the way the cowboys were crowding around, they considered it a fair exchange.

Cambridge swung down from the saddle and hitched his horse with the others. As he made his way toward the tables, he took off his hat and nodded to the ladies he passed. A man in a black broadcloth suit and a string tie popped up in front of him, and Cambridge knew he had just encountered the local preacher.

"Good day, brother," the minister said heartily, extending his right hand. The left held a Bible. "Glad you could join our little get-together. I'm John Livingston."

"Billy Cambridge," the lawyer replied, shaking hands with Livingston. The preacher had a firm grip.

"I don't believe I've seen you around here before, Mr. Cambridge. Were you just passing through the area when you heard about our regular Wednesday lunch?"

"Actually, I came here looking for somebody, Reverend. Jake Maxwell over at the stagecoach station told me I might find Deputy Gilliam here."

Livingston frowned for a second. "I hope there's no trouble. . . ." he began.

"I just need to talk to the deputy for a few minutes," Cambridge said quickly. "If he's here, could you point him out to me?"

"Of course." Livingston turned halfway around and pointed toward a man who was already seated under one of the trees, a plate heaped high with food perched on his knees. "That's Bart over there."

Cambridge nodded. "Much obliged."

As he started to turn away, Livingston said, "Mr. Cambridge . . . I notice you're wearing a gun. We really don't like having people carry firearms at these meetings. Most of the men leave them with their horses or on their wagons."

"Sorry, Reverend. I didn't know." Cambridge went back to his horse, taking off the gunbelt along the way. He coiled it over the saddle horn, thinking that it should be safe there. It wasn't likely anybody would try to steal something right here in front of a church.

Bart Gilliam was a man in his mid-thirties, Cambridge saw as he walked up to the deputy. Gilliam's battered black hat was cuffed back on his head, revealing a thatch of rumpled brown hair. He was gnawing on a chicken leg. His front teeth were large and yellow, with a sizable gap between them.

"Deputy Gilliam?" Cambridge asked.

Gilliam looked up and grinned. "That's me," he admitted. "Somethin' I can do for you, mister?"

"I want to report a robbery."

"Awww . . ." The deputy sounded disappointed. "You're joshin' me, ain't you?"

"I'm afraid not. The northbound stagecoach that passed through these parts yesterday afternoon was stopped, and the passengers' valuables were stolen."

Gilliam put the chicken leg back on his plate and sighed. "Shoot. What'd you say your name was, mister?"

"I didn't say, but it's Billy Cambridge. I'm an attorney, and I was one of the passengers who was robbed. I'd like to know what you intend to do about it."

Standing up and brushing off the seat of his pants, Gilliam asked, "You got any idea who the owlhoots were, Mr. Cambridge?"

"None at all. But Jake Maxwell at the Red River stage station said that a gang of outlaws has been operating in this area lately. I'd say there's a good chance the same bunch held us up. They headed southwest."

"Yep, they usually do," the deputy nodded. "Well, I'll tell the sheriff 'bout the hold-up. That's all I can do right now."

Cambridge took a deep breath and suppressed the surge of anger he felt at Gilliam's lackadaisical attitude. "You're not going to try to trail those criminals?"

Gilliam grimaced and rubbed at his beard-stubbled jaw. "Can't very well do that. The sheriff's got to authorize all posses. All I can do is turn the information over to him."

"All right," Cambridge sighed. Maxwell had been right: if anybody was going to catch the outlaws and recover that stolen money, he and Nacho were going to have to do it themselves.

"'Preciate you bringin' this to the law's attention," Gilliam went on, reaching for his plate again. "You bein' a lawyer and all, you probably wouldn't believe how many folks around here seem to figure they can just take the law in their own hands."

Cambridge didn't say anything. But having just seen an example of how the local authorities operated, he had no trouble believing it at all.

By late morning, Nacho was feeling restless. He might not be able to ride a horse, but that didn't mean he had to sit on his rear end all day. When Jake Maxwell came into the building from doing some chores, Nacho asked him, "Does your son's trading post sell guns? I don't feel right with an empty holster."

Maxwell nodded. "Sure, Ted—I mean Theodore—has some guns for sale. You ought to be able to find a pistol that suits you. Or I might could scare up one to loan to you, like I did with Billy."

"No, thanks," Nacho said with a shake of his head. "I'd feel better with a gun of my own." He scowled. "Except I just remembered I don't have any money. Those masked hombres took all I had."

"Don't worry about that," Maxwell assured him. "You tell my boy I'll stand good for the gun. You can pay me back whenever you get a chance, Nacho."

The foreman grinned. "That's mighty nice of you, Mr. Maxwell. I could understand if it was Billy, since the two of you are old friends . . ."

"I'm not worried about the money. And call me Jake. I feel old enough without being called Mr. Maxwell all the time."

"All right, Jake. *Muchas gracias.* I'll go over there now and pick out a gun."

"Won't be long until lunch time," Maxwell reminded him. "It's just stew again, but I reckon that's better than nothing."

"Much better." Nacho grinned. "I will be here, don't worry."

He picked up his hat and walked out of the station building. Outside, the sun shone warm on his face, and it felt good. The crisp, clean air felt even better. Nacho strolled across the gap separating the stage station and the trading post, wondering if he would see the lovely Sandra Maxwell again.

The attractive young blonde was nowhere in sight as he climbed the steps to the porch of the trading post, then went through the open double doors into the building. The smell inside was unmistakable. A trading post such as this one carried almost as wide a variety of goods as did the general mercantiles located in towns, only in smaller quantities. The aroma was a blend of coffee, spices, tobacco, leather, horse liniment, vinegar from the pickle barrel, and dust. The shelves along the aisles in the center of the building held crockery and cutlery, hardware, bolts of cloth, boots and shoes, and a few ready-made shirts and pants. Sawhorses sat along the right-hand wall with saddles perched on them, while harnesses, bridles, and assorted pieces of tack hung on pegs on the wall above them.

On the left-hand wall was a glass-fronted counter, and the shelves under it were filled with candy and gaudy jewelry. Nacho spotted the guns in the back, arranged in another of the glass display cases. As he came closer, he saw there was an assortment of handguns, rifles, and shotguns in it.

There didn't seem to be anybody around. Nacho frowned as he leaned over and studied the weapons arranged in the display case. It wasn't very common for folks to go off and leave a well-stocked trading post like this unattended.

He had settled on a Colt Single Action Army revolver like the one he had lost to the outlaws when he heard voices coming from behind a door on the other side of the counter. Nacho wasn't the eavesdropping sort, but the words were loud and angry and hard to miss.

"I don't believe you," a man said heatedly. "You might as well tell me where you went, Sandra. I know you've been sneaking out at night!"

"Don't be ridiculous. I haven't been anywhere except here at the trading post or over at the stage station in weeks."

That was Sandra Maxwell's voice, all right, Nacho thought, and the man arguing with her was no doubt her husband Theodore. Nacho's frown deepened. Why anybody would want to exchange harsh words with such a beauty was beyond him. Women like Sandra were meant for softly whispered messages of romance, of moonlight and gentle breezes—

Nacho grimaced and forced that train of thought out of his head. He had no business thinking such things about a married woman. But from the sound of what was going on in the back room of the trading post, Sandra's marriage was not a happy one, at least not at the moment.

"Don't lie to me!" Theodore Maxwell snapped. "I woke up last night and you were gone. Didn't know that, did you?" Sandra let out a little gasp of pain and surprise as Theodore went on, "Dammit, tell me the truth! Where the hell were you?"

Nacho straightened sharply. There had been no sound of a blow, so Theodore hadn't slapped his wife, but he could have grabbed her roughly and shaken her. That would have caused her reaction.

He couldn't go behind the counter and barge into that back room, whether he wanted to or not. What went on between a man and his wife was their personal business, and an outsider had no right to interfere. That was what Nacho had always believed. But it was becoming more difficult to stand here and listen to the argument without becoming involved.

"Let go of me!" Sandra exclaimed, confirming Nacho's guess about what was going on, and he took an involuntary step toward the door leading into the rear before he stopped himself. Quickly, he turned on his heel and strode soundlessly to the front of the store.

When he reached the doors, he turned again, this time letting his steps thump heavily on the broad planks of the floor. "Anybody here?" he called loudly.

For a moment, there was no response, but then the door to the back room creaked open. A man stepped out, stared along the length of the building at Nacho, and asked, "What can I do for you, mister?"

"I'm looking for Mr. Theodore Maxwell." Nacho started forward as he spoke.

"That's me."

Nacho walked up to the counter. "Pleased to meet you, *señor.* I'm Nacho Graves. I'm staying over at the stage station with your father, and I'm in need of a new pistol. Jake said he would take care of the cost for the time being, since I am, ah, without funds at the moment."

Theodore regarded his customer with a suspicious stare. He was a few years younger than Nacho, but there was something old-looking about his eyes. He was clean-shaven and had the same thick dark hair as his father. His mouth was set in what Nacho feared might be a perpetually sour expression. He wore a tan work shirt and the same sort of bibbed apron worn by storekeepers all over the West.

"My father said he'd buy you a gun?" Theodore asked in disbelief. "I'm going to have to ask him about that, mister. And if I find out you're lying, I won't appreciate it."

Nacho kept a tight rein on his temper. "You go ahead and do that, friend," he told Theodore. "I just left him over at the station."

Theodore started to come out from behind the counter, but he stopped when Sandra emerged from the back room. She smiled when she saw Nacho and said, "Good morning, Mr. Graves. How are you feeling today?"

Nacho quickly tugged his hat off. "Better, ma'am, thank you. I came to look at your guns. Jake said he would loan me the price of a pistol."

"I'm sure that would be fine." Sandra turned to her husband, and there was no sign in her expression or voice that they had just been fighting as she went on, "Mr. Graves is traveling with an old friend of Father's, Theodore. You've heard him speak about Billy Cambridge. They were in the Rangers together."

Theodore nodded curtly. "Yeah, I guess so. That sounds familiar. I don't listen to all of the old man's stories anymore. You get tired of them after a while." He waved a hand and indicated the guns in the display case. "Pick out whatever you want, Graves. Just don't take off for the tall and uncut until *somebody* pays me for it."

"*Gracias*," Nacho muttered, wondering if Theodore Maxwell had to work at being such an unpleasant bastard. From what he had seen of the man's father, the trait wasn't inherited.

Even though he had already made up his mind which gun he wanted, he made a show of studying them for several moments before pointing out the Colt he had selected. Theodore took it out from under the counter and handed it to Nacho. He hefted the gun, checking its balance and the feel of its grips against his palm, then nodded in satisfaction. In the meantime, Sandra was moving around the store, straightening and dusting merchandise. Nacho glanced at her out of the corner of his eye and saw that she was moving stiffly, as if the anger she had covered up with a bright smile was being expressed instead by a rigid spine.

"This will do fine," Nacho told Theodore as he slipped the revolver into his empty holster. The fit was as close to perfect as a new gun could get. "I'll need a box of forty-fives, too."

Theodore slid the cartridges across the counter. "I suppose my father is paying for these, too," he commented sarcastically.

"I will pay him back," Nacho declared, finding it more and more difficult to hold his temper.

"I hope you do."

Nacho's fingers tightened on the box of bullets, but he didn't say anything more to Theodore. Turning to Sandra, he tipped his hat again and said, "Good day to you, ma'am."

"Good day to you, Mr. Graves. . . . Oh, would you tell Jake that I've gathered the eggs, and I'll bring some over to him later?"

"Sure."

They had probably been out in the little barn behind the trading post when he first came in, Nacho thought. Sandra had gone out there to gather the eggs, and Theodore had followed to harangue her about his suspicions.

He listened closely as he left the building, wondering if Theodore was going to start in on his wife again. Nacho hoped that wouldn't be the case. It was difficult to leave, knowing that Theodore might become even more obnoxious as soon as he was gone.

Nacho sighed. He had done all he could, distracting Theodore for a few minutes that way and in the process sparing Sandra the embarrassment of knowing that the argument had been overheard. She'd had the chance to leave the trading post on some excuse while he was there, and since she hadn't taken it, she probably wasn't that frightened of her husband.

Blowhards like Theodore would usually back off in a hurry once somebody stood up to them. Sandra would do that when she got tired enough of his unwarranted suspicions, Nacho told himself.

At the moment, he had other concerns on his mind. He felt better now that he was armed again, but instead of calming his restlessness, the visit to the trading post had only increased it. As soon as Billy thought it would be all right, he wanted to be on the back of a horse, tracking down the men who had raided the stagecoach.

He wouldn't feel right until that score was settled.

Chapter Four

Billy Cambridge accepted the hospitality of the Baptist ladies and stayed for lunch. He had told Jake Maxwell before leaving the stage station earlier that he might not be back in time for the noon meal, so he assumed that Jake and Nacho would go ahead and eat without him. The food was good, especially out-of-doors on a pleasant autumn day, and Cambridge tried not to let Bart Gilliam annoy him. The deputy kept casting resentful glances toward him, like he was angry that Cambridge had disturbed his meal with the news of fresh lawbreaking.

Cambridge was sitting on a bench next to one of the heavily laden tables when John Livingston walked over and sat down beside him. "I hope you're enjoying your meal, Mr. Cambridge," he said.

"It's excellent, pastor. If I, ah, had any money at the moment, I'd feel moved to make a donation to the church."

Livingston waved away the offer. "Don't worry about that. These meals are free for any who care to partake. And if you're short of money, the church has a sort of fund to help out those in need. . . ."

Cambridge shook his head quickly. "That's not it at all. You see, I was robbed yesterday. I was on the northbound stage when outlaws stopped it and held us up."

"I see." Livingston smiled slightly. "I was wondering what you had to say to Deputy Gilliam that disturbed him so. Now I understand. You wanted him to actually do some law enforcement work."

"I take it you don't have a very high opinion of the deputy."

"Don't misunderstand me. Bart is a good man, an honest man. So is Sheriff Massey. But they don't seem to be able to find the gang that's been wreaking havoc around here for the past few months." The minister shrugged. "I don't hold that against them. They're doing their best."

"Well, that's not good enough. I lost a considerable amount of money that belongs to a client of mine in that robbery. I plan to get it back before I go on to Fort Smith. That's where I was heading with a friend."

Livingston stood up and held out his hand. As Cambridge shook it, the pastor said, "I wish you good luck in your quest, Mr. Cambridge. I'm no manhunter, but if I can help you in any way, please let me know."

"I'll do that, Reverend," Cambridge promised.

He finished his meal, conveyed his thanks to the ladies of the church, then headed for his horse. As he walked toward the hitch rack where several other mounts were tied, he suddenly heard hoofbeats to his left. Glancing up, he saw a buggy rolling rapidly toward him as the woman at the reins tried to control the skittish horse pulling the vehicle.

Cambridge quickly stepped back out of the way, and as the horse danced past him, he reached up and grabbed the animal's bridle. He hauled down on it, stopping the horse short and bringing it under control. "Hold on there, boy," he said soothingly.

"Thank you," the woman called from the seat of the buggy. "I didn't mean to nearly run you down, mister. I don't know how the horse got away from me like that." She tightened up on the reins gripped in her slender fingers to prevent another such incident.

"That's all right," Cambridge told her. "I'm just glad I was here to grab him before he got too wound up."

The woman nodded. Cambridge couldn't see her face very well, since it was partially concealed by a large sun bonnet, but she seemed to be young. The lithe figure in her calico dress was that of a young woman, at any rate.

"I can handle it now," she told him. "Thanks again."

Cambridge let go of the horse's bridle and stepped back. He tipped his hat as the woman drove the buggy past him, and she turned her head enough to give him a smile. The glimpse he got of her features was a quick one, but it confirmed his impression. She was no more than twenty, with skin the color of honey. Her eyes were dark and flashing, and the only thing that detracted from her beauty was a scar of some sort running horizontally across her left cheek. Cambridge didn't get a good look at it, since that side of her face was turned away from him for the most part. As she passed, he saw the long, straight, raven-black hair hanging down her back.

Frowning slightly as he watched the buggy roll away from the church, Cambridge wondered who the girl was. He hadn't noticed her around the tables while he was eating or talking to Deputy Gilliam. As striking as she was, he would have remembered seeing her. He must have just missed her somehow, because from her garb it was obvious that she was one of the ladies from the church. Some of the others were leaving now, as this weekly dinner was coming to an end.

With a smile, Cambridge shook his head. He didn't have time to waste thinking about a pretty girl. That was more in Nacho's line. He had some outlaws to locate. Strapping his gunbelt on again when he reached his horse, he prepared to swing up into the saddle.

But for some reason, he glanced one more time in the direction the girl's buggy had gone. It had disappeared from sight by now, of course, but the image of her face, brief though it had been, was still vivid in Cambridge's mind. For a second, he considered asking Reverend Livingston about her. . . .

Then he told himself he was being ridiculous and headed back toward the Red River station.

Nacho was waiting on the porch when the lawyer rode into the clearing in front of the station. He was perched on a straight chair that was leaned back against the wall. With his pocket knife, he was carving a chunk of wood into an unrecognizable shape.

"Billy!" Nacho called out as Cambridge rode up. He tossed down the wood and closed his knife. "I been waiting for you to get back. You find out anything?"

Cambridge dismounted and looped the reins over the railing along the porch. "Not much," he admitted. "The outlaws headed southwest, like the driver said, and the local law doesn't seem to be very efficient, like Jake said. So, other than confirming that, I didn't accomplish a thing." Cambridge forced a weary smile. "How are you feeling this afternoon?"

"I'm a lot better," Nacho told him. "I think I could ride right now if I had to, and I know I'll be able to by tomorrow."

With a dubious frown, Cambridge said, "I don't know about that. It was just yesterday afternoon you were shot, for God's sake! You don't need to get in too big a hurry, Nacho, or you'll wind up hurt worse than you were before."

Nacho grimaced. He had been afraid Cambridge would react that way. "You don't understand, Billy. I can't sit around here for days. There's nothing to do! I was *whittling* when you rode up. You ever known me to whittle before?"

"Well . . . I don't reckon I've ever *seen* you whittling until now."

"I am a man of action!" Nacho said, clenching a fist for emphasis. "If I sit around, I will turn into a . . . a codger, like the old men who sit on benches in town and play dominoes. You don't want that to happen, do you, Billy?"

Cambridge chuckled. "No, I wouldn't want that to happen. But give it at least another day, Nacho. Surely you can stand it that long."

"I suppose so," Nacho said with a sigh. "But I'm ready to start tracking down those skunks who robbed us."

"So am I, Nacho, so am I." Cambridge looked around. "Where's Jake?"

Nacho jerked a thumb over his shoulder. "I think he said he was going out to the barn."

"Thanks. I want to pick his brain a little about that country to the southwest. It's been a long time since I rode through any of it. We need to be prepared before we take out after those men."

Nacho nodded as Cambridge walked away. When the attorney had disappeared around the corner of the building, Nacho's forehead creased with worry. He hadn't told Cambridge the whole truth. He was anxious to find those desperados and recover the stolen money, of course, because he still felt like he had let Cambridge and Edward Nash down. But he had another reason for wanting to go on to Fort Smith and leave this stage station behind. Ever since his encounter that morning with Theodore and Sandra Maxwell, an uneasy feeling had been gnawing on Nacho's belly. There was trouble in the making here, and he didn't want any part of it.

But he wasn't sure he would be able to stay uninvolved, not if Theodore had had anything to do with that bruise he had seen on Sandra's jaw the night before.

Nacho had been born in the wilds of West Texas in the early days of

40

its settlement, when women were few and far between. As a result, he had grown up with the idea that females were to be protected and cherished. To Nacho's way of thinking, any man who would strike a woman was just asking for a beating, at the very least.

He wasn't sure how to go about explaining all of this to Cambridge, though. Billy might be reluctant to believe the worst about the son of his old comrade. But Cambridge hadn't met Theodore yet, either.

Nacho sighed again. This trip had turned out to be more complicated than he had ever thought it would be. It had sounded so simple at first—deliver the money to Fort Smith, see some country he hadn't seen before, take advantage of the opportunity to ride a stagecoach, a means of transportation that might soon be vanishing from the West.

Instead he'd gone through a robbery, been shot, and landed in a situation that was just boiling with potential trouble.

He wished he was back on the ranch near Pecos. Punching cows had this beat all to hell.

A southbound stage was due to come through that afternoon, and Jake Maxwell was making his usual check of the horses that would make up the fresh team. Their shoes were in good shape, and they appeared to be rested and ready to go. He picked up a brush and was running it over the flank of one of the animals when he heard the light footsteps behind him.

He didn't have to turn around to know who the visitor was. He would recognize that sound anywhere, not to mention the delicate scent of lilac water that accompanied his daughter-in-law.

"Hello, Sandra," he said.

"Hello, Jake. I brought you some eggs. I left them in the station, just inside the back door."

"Thanks." Maxwell glanced over his shoulder and saw her standing between him and the open barn door, the sunlight behind her making her long blond hair glow as it fell around her face and shoulders. She looked like something that should have been in a picture. He turned, unable to take his eyes off her.

He had known Sandra ever since she was a little girl, growing up on her father's farm several miles east of the station. She had grown into a real beauty, and he had been surprised when his son Ted had wound up marrying her. Sandra could have had any young man for miles around—all of them had paid court to her at one time or another since she turned fourteen—but she had chosen Ted, who had never been a particularly handsome boy. Ted didn't have much charm about him, either; most of the time he was rather dour. Maxwell knew he shouldn't think such things about his own son, but damn it, they were the truth.

Maxwell had wondered briefly if Sandra had married Ted because she'd found out somehow that the trading post was going to be his. It was hard to credit that, though. Maxwell hadn't even told Ted about his decision to turn over the trading post until after the wedding. Besides, once he got to know Sandra, he was convinced that such scheming would never occur to her. She was too open and good-hearted for that. And, if she'd wanted to marry for money, she could have done better than Ted.

The only thing Maxwell could come up with was that for whatever reasons she might have, Sandra honestly loved his son.

Or at least she did when she married him.

Now she took a step closer to Maxwell and said, "I saw Mr. Graves over at the post this morning. He picked out a gun and some shells and said you'd pay for them."

"That's right," Maxwell nodded. "Reckon I'd better go over there and take care of that. I imagine Ted's startin' to get worried about it."

"You know Theodore. . . . he's always worried about money."

Maxwell grunted. He knew his son, all right. Sometimes he thought he knew him too well. He loved Ted, of course—there was enough of the boy's mother in him that Maxwell couldn't help but love him—but sometimes he wasn't sure he liked him. He certainly didn't like the way Ted sometimes treated Sandra, snapping at her, bossing her around, maybe—worse.

"I'll get over there as soon as I can. I'd best wait until after the southbound's come through, though."

"I'll tell Theodore."

Maxwell nodded, and as he did, his eyes strayed down to the thrust of Sandra's breasts against the fabric of her dress. His mind strayed as well, distracted from their idle chatting by the rise and fall of her bosom as she breathed. Damn, but the girl was lovely . . . !

With a sharp intake of breath, Maxwell tore his gaze away from her body. He had no right to be looking at her like that, and he knew it. His face flushing with shame, he turned back to the horses and told himself he was nothing but a lecherous old man to be staring at his own daughter-in-law's breasts like that. "Got to get busy," he grunted without looking at her again.

"All right," Sandra said slowly. Her voice shook slightly, and he could tell that she was upset, too. Well, she had every right to be! She probably thought he was disgusting. After a moment, she went on, "I'll see you later, Jake."

"Sure." He kept his tone flat and expressionless.

He stood there waiting as she left the barn, then dragged a deep breath into his lungs. There was no excuse for letting the girl affect him like that. He was old enough to be her father, after all. He'd been married for over twenty years, been a widower for nearly ten. He should have been long past having his head turned by a pretty young woman, even one as lovely as Sandra.

The worst part about it was that this wasn't the first time such a thing had happened. It seemed like the worse Ted treated Sandra, the more Maxwell felt himself drawn to her. At first he had told himself what he was feeling was just the normal sympathy any man would feel under those circumstances. But as time passed and he found himself looking at her more and more, he realized that wasn't the case. It was a sobering, shocking revelation, and he'd spent many long, sleepless nights railing at himself for the evil thoughts that were invading his brain.

Sandra knew how he felt, he was sure of that. She had caught him staring at her enough times, just like today, that she had to be aware of what was going on. The whole thing might have been easier to deal with if she had just gone ahead and slapped his face or spat on him in disgust.

But the only emotion he had ever seen in her eyes at those times wasn't shame or anger or embarrassment. It was . . . sadness.

Those thoughts raced through Maxwell's mind in the moment after Sandra left the barn. He let out the deep breath in a weary sigh, then stiffened as he heard her voice outside, between the barn and the station building. "Hello, Mr. Cambridge," she said. "Jake's in the barn, if you're looking for him."

"Thanks, ma'am," Billy Cambridge replied. "That's who I'm looking for, all right."

Maxwell turned around as Cambridge came into the barn. He lifted a hand in greeting and said, "Howdy, Billy. You find what you were lookin' for?"

"I found Deputy Gilliam," Cambridge replied. "You were right about where he'd be, Jake. And you were right about his attitude, too. He said he'd report the hold-up to the sheriff, but that was all he was willing to do."

"And Massey'll cluck his tongue and make a note and stick it in his desk, and that'll be the end of it," Maxwell told him. "You find any tracks on the road?"

Cambridge nodded. "They took off southwest, into the breaks. That's no surprise."

"Nope. Lots more places to hide out over there than there would be anywhere else around here. Too much open farmland to the south and east. Of course, they could've gone north and crossed the Red into Indian Territory. Plenty of owlhoots up there, from what I hear." Maxwell stuck his hands in his pockets. "But up there they'd have to worry about those deputy marshals Judge Parker sends out from Fort Smith. Reckon you've heard about Parker?"

"The Hanging Judge? I've heard about him, all right. I hope to be able to pay him a call while I'm in Fort Smith—if I ever get there."

"You'll get there—Maxwell said with a grin—"and you'll have that money with you. I never knew Billy Cambridge to let go of something once he got his teeth into it."

"I'm getting older," Cambridge pointed out. "My teeth may not be as strong as they used to be." He shook his head. "What I really want to know is whether or not that country to the southwest is as rugged as it used to be."

Maxwell hooked a three-legged stool with the toe of his boot, pulled it over, and gestured for Cambridge to sit down. He upended a bucket and used it for his own seat. "It's rugged, all right," he said, glad for the excuse to get his mind off Sandra. Leaning forward, Maxwell traced a wavering line in the dirt with his fingertip. "That's the Red River." He drew another line branching southwest. "That's the Wichita. There's a few little towns between here and Wichita Falls, like Ringgold, but they don't amount to much. Some folks have moved in and started farms and ranches over there. They're wide-scattered, though. Mostly the country's brush-choked gullies and rocky little hills, except for that flat stretch where the Chisholm Trail runs."

"What's the Trail like these days?"

"Folks don't use it much anymore, not since the Texas & Pacific reached Fort Worth in '76. The days of the big cattle drives to Kansas are over,

Billy. I reckon the Trail will be flattened out and dusty for a long time, but the day'll come when you can look over the land and never be able to tell it was there."

Cambridge shook his head. "Times are changing, that's for sure. That's one reason I decided to take the stagecoach to Arkansas. I figure it won't be much longer until the stages aren't running anymore."

"You're right. The company keeps complainin' about how people don't take the stage, and then they cut their rates again. Ain't goin' to matter how cheap they make the tickets, though. Nobody's goin' to want to spend weeks in a hot, dusty stagecoach gettin' their teeth rattled out when they can make the same trip in days on a train, and in a lot more comfort to boot."

"What will you do when the stage line closes down?" Cambridge asked.

"Keep on raisin' horses. It's about the only thing I know how to do. This place is mine; the company just leases it." Maxwell grinned. "Don't worry, Billy. I'll make out just fine. Anyway, the stagecoach ain't on its last legs just yet. It'll be around for a while."

"I hope so," Cambridge said. He leaned forward, a solemn look on his face, and went on, "Do you think we'll be able to follow the trail those owlhoots left?"

"Well, that all depends. As I recall, you ain't the best tracker these parts have ever seen, Billy."

Cambridge gave a little laugh. "No, I'm not, but Nacho Graves may be. His father was British and he can act as civilized as he wants to, but inside he's all *vaquero.*"

"You've got a chance, then. It hasn't rained in the last couple of days, and I'm not expectin' any for a few more days. Ought to still be some tracks you can follow."

"What if we lose the trail, though? Do you have any idea where a gang like that might be holed up?"

"Hard to say," Maxwell replied with a shake of his head. "There are abandoned cabins scattered all through that country, where folks tried to make a go of a ranch or a farm and failed. You might stop and talk to a man named O'Shea. He's got a place a ways west of here, and if anybody knows what's going on out there in the breaks, it'd be him."

The lawyer nodded. "O'Shea. I'll remember that."

"Him and me, we're not what you'd call close friends, but we know each other to nod to. You might mention my name if you talk to him."

"All right. Thanks." Cambridge paused for a moment, then said, "Is something bothering you, Jake? You're starting to look like you're going to cloud up and rain."

"I was just thinkin' about you and Nacho goin' after them bandits by yourself," Maxwell said slowly. "What are you goin' to do if you find 'em? You said there was a half a dozen of 'em in that robbery, and there could be more in the gang. You and Nacho are just two men."

Cambridge's expression was solemn as he replied, "I know. We can't hope to capture them by ourselves. Trying a stunt like that would just get us killed. But if we could find their hide-out, then we could take the law back there. Surely even this Sheriff Massey would send out a posse—if we could tell him exactly where to find the gang."

"Maybe, maybe not," Maxwell said doubtfully.

"Well, what about the Rangers? They'd help if they had solid evidence."

"That might be your best bet. I just wouldn't want to see you and Nacho tryin' to bring those bastards in by yourselves."

Cambridge laughed shortly. "Don't worry. I'm mad, Jake, but I'm not crazy. We wouldn't face them down unless we happened to run into two or three of them by themselves. And then we'd probably think twice."

Maxwell stood up. "Glad to hear it," he said, brushing off the seat of his pants. He took his watch from his pocket and flipped it open to check the time. "I got a southbound stage scheduled to come through pretty soon, so I'd best get these fresh horses ready to go."

"Thanks for the information," Cambridge said as he got to his feet. "And for all your help. I don't know what we would have done without you."

"You'd have figured out something else," Maxwell said, slapping his old friend on the back. "You always were the thinkin'est son-of-a-buck I ever knew, Billy."

Cambridge chuckled again and left the barn, strolling back toward the station building. Maxwell watched him go, and the smile dropped off the stationmaster's face as Cambridge disappeared into the building. It had been good to see Billy again, damn good, but Maxwell hoped that Cambridge was able to conclude his business and move on. Cambridge was smart and he knew how to keep his eyes open; Maxwell would hate like the dickens for Cambridge to discover what was going on around here. He'd never live down the shame if his old friend were to find out how he felt about Sandra.

And just like that, there she was again. Not in the flesh this time, but her face and her body filled his mind's eye anyway. He had been able to keep his thoughts away from her for a few minutes, but that seemed to be the limit.

If this kept up, he wasn't going to have any choice about what to do next.

He would have to leave the Red River station before something happened that could never be forgiven. Before he did something that would tear apart the fragile shreds of honor and self-respect that he had left. . . .

Chapter Five

Theodore was nowhere in sight when Sandra came back into the trading post, and she felt a surge of relief. But as soon as she did, a feeling of disloyalty came over her, and she caught at her bottom lip, worrying it between her even white teeth.

Her husband was gone a great deal those days, and Sandra had no idea where he was spending his time. She didn't care. When he wasn't home, at least he wasn't tormenting her.

She almost felt like laughing whenever she thought about the situation. Theodore was constantly accusing her of sneaking around and keeping things from him, but he was the one who was usually missing. He was the one who had secrets. And he became violent whenever she dared to question him about his comings and goings.

It hadn't always been that way. When she had first met him, he had been . . . well, not charming, perhaps, but at least likable. And friendly, that was another good word to describe Theodore Maxwell.

Lord, it hadn't taken long for *that* to change.

It had started with Theodore insisting that he wasn't good enough for her. He had constantly talked about someday having more money, as if that would justify her affection for him. He wanted her love, wanted it with a need bordering on desperation, but he didn't seem to know how to go about keeping it. Sandra had never cared that much about money. If that was all she was interested in when it came to men, she could have picked richer suitors.

The jealousy popped up soon after Theodore's obsession with wealth. He wanted her to account for every minute of her time, which wasn't difficult. She hardly ever went anywhere, other than next door to the stage station.

She didn't know what she would have done without Jake.

She'd known Jake even longer than she had known Theodore; the stationmaster had been acquainted with her father. Growing up, Jake Maxwell had been almost like an uncle to her, and that was one reason she was willing to marry Theodore. If the son was anything like the father, she had reasoned, it would be a good marriage.

But Theodore wasn't like Jake at all, and she had found herself relying on her father-in-law for friendship. He was like a rock she could hang on to for support while she tried to sort out the unexpected twists and turns of her life.

And then things got even more complicated. Jake began looking at her not like a father-in-law looks at his son's wife, but rather the way a man looks at a woman—a woman he desires.

The worst part about it, Sandra found herself thinking more than once, was that she didn't mind. Didn't mind at all.

At first she had simply been flattered, but then she discovered that she was starting to regard Jake in the same light: as a man, not just as her father-in-law. He was quite a bit older than her, that was true, but he was healthy and vigorous and looked younger than he was, probably because he led an active life. He was kind and considerate and genuinely fond of her, she was sure of that.

As incredible as it seemed to her at times, she was beginning to realize that she had married the wrong Maxwell.

Sandra spent the afternoon brooding over the situation, hardly speaking to the customers who came into the trading post. She knew she was being impolite, but the latest encounter with Jake, when he had looked so hungrily at her in the barn, was consuming her thoughts. When Theodore finally wandered in, late in the afternoon, she hardly looked up at him.

But she did ask, "Where have you been?"

That was a mistake, and she knew it even as she spoke the words. But she supposed she was in the mood for a fight. She wouldn't let him hit her this time, she knew that. Before she would allow that, she would reach for the loaded shotgun he kept under the counter in the rear of the store. Not even Theodore was foolish enough to advance in the face of a loaded greener.

"That's none of your damned business," he replied peevishly as he came behind the counter. "You don't tell me about your comings and goings. I don't see why I should tell you about mine."

That was a more reasonable response than she usually got from him these days. She prodded him again. "There's no secrets about where I go. You're the one who's hiding something, Theodore."

"You're crazy," he said without looking at her. "I've known it from the first. I never should have married you."

"You're probably right," she sniffed contemptuously.

She was being foolish and she knew it, but her wounded emotions wouldn't let her stop. She kept pressing him on his whereabouts during the afternoon, following him from one end of the trading post to the other while he tried to take a rough inventory of their goods, until he abruptly threw down the pencil and piece of paper he was using to jot down figures. Whirling toward her, he grabbed her arms.

Sandra gasped. She was nowhere near the shotgun under the counter. She'd let herself be trapped, and now there was no telling what he would do to her.

"Shut up!" he said brokenly. "I'm tired of listening to you!" He shook her as he spoke. "You keep your pretty little nose out of my business, or you'll be sorry, Sandra. I can promise you that."

Thankfully, he hadn't struck her. She tried to pull away from him, but his fingers tightened painfully on her shoulders. "Let me go!" she cried.

He jerked her closer, until his breath was hot in her face. "Not yet. Not until you understand. Maybe I'm not man enough for you anymore, maybe I never was. But you're damn well going to have to make the best of it." He drew a deep, ragged breath. "Someday, you'll feel differently about me. When I'm a rich, important man, maybe you won't think you made such a mistake by marrying me!"

It wouldn't do any good to tell him that her mistake wasn't in marrying a man who wasn't rich; what she had done wrong was to pick a man for her mate who was unbalanced. She was growing more convinced every day that Theodore was insane.

She stood stock-still, his hands digging into her shoulders, tears filming her eyes and threatening to brim over and roll down her cheeks. She didn't want him to see her crying. She blinked furiously, trying to drive the moisture away.

Finally, he released her with a little shove and curtly turned away. Sandra bit back the sigh of relief she felt welling up inside her. Theodore stalked to the front door and left the building. As soon as he was gone, Sandra was able to breathe again. She turned to one of the shelves in the center of the store, rested her palms on it, and let her head sag as she tried to quiet the turmoil inside her.

A few minutes later, a soft, tentative footstep made her look up. Jake Maxwell stood in the doorway, one foot inside the store, the other still on the porch. He frowned and asked, "What's wrong, Sandy? I just saw Ted come out of here lookin' like a mad 'possum."

Sandra shook her head. "It's nothing for you to worry about, Jake. Just a little disagreement."

"Seems like you and that boy of mine've been havin' them disagreements pretty regular." Jake came a few steps closer. He took a deep breath, hesitated, then blurted, "He didn't hit you this time, did he?"

Her head snapped up. "How did you. . . . She managed to break off the question before finishing it, but it was too late. Jake knew quite well what she had been about to ask.

"How'd I know? Shoot, I'm not blind, girl." He stepped up to her and put a hand on her arm. "I'll have a talk with him." His voice was grim. "I'll straighten him out. I'm his father. I've got a right . . ."

"No." Sandra caught at her father-in-law's sleeve. "Please don't get mixed up in this, Jake. Theodore's changed. He's not like he used to be."

"He's still my son, and I won't have him mistreatin' somebody as fine as you."

A bleak smile tugged at her mouth. "He doesn't think I'm fine."

"Son or not, the boy's a fool," Jake said quietly.

Sandra looked up at him. His hand was still on her arm, and she was clutching his sleeve. After a long moment, she said, "Thank you, Jake. I . . . I don't know what I would have done. . . .

"Hush." He put his arm around her and folded her against him. "Just hush now. It'll be all right."

Sandra didn't know how long they stood there like that. The moment seemed to last forever, and yet it was over much too soon when Jake finally let her go and stepped back.

"Reckon you'll be all right now?" he asked.

She nodded and wiped away a few errant tears. "I'll be fine," she told him. "Thank you, Jake."

"Glad to help," he said gruffly. He started to turn away.

Sandra lifted her hand. She was all too aware of how she had felt while she was in his arms. She had felt safe and protected, of course, but there had been more to it than that.

She had wanted him to hold her forever.

And if she touched him again now, with the emotions that were coursing through both of them, they might not be able to back away this time. The thing that had been haunting both of them might come stampeding right out into the open.

Sandra couldn't stop herself. Her fingertips lightly brushed his shoulder.

Jake stopped in his tracks. He didn't look at her. A shudder ran through his shoulders, visible evidence of the indecision that was gripping him. He might still be able to walk away from her, she sensed, unless she communicated with him somehow that this was what she wanted.

She whispered his name.

He turned sharply, his hands reaching out to grasp her upper arms. They pulled her toward him, but unlike Theodore, this was a gentle urging. Sandra came willingly, pressing herself against him as his mouth started toward hers.

One last time, he stopped. Jake Maxwell had always been a good man. There had been some wild times in his past—nobody had ever mistaken the Texas frontier for a Sunday School—but there were lines he had never crossed.

Until now.

He kissed his daughter-in-law.

Sandra molded herself into his embrace. She felt her own pulse hammering in her head, and she felt the beat of his heart against her. Her lips opened under his.

Right away, she knew she'd never been kissed like this. Theodore hardly ever kissed her, even when they were in bed.

She shoved thoughts of Theodore out of her head, not even worrying that he might return and find her in his father's arms. Whenever they had an argument and he stomped out like that, he was always gone at least an hour. As usual, she had no idea where he went, but she didn't care. As long as he wasn't here . . .

This moment really could have lasted forever, as far as she was concerned.

What the *hell* was he doing? Jake Maxwell asked himself.

Well, the answer was simple enough, he supposed. He was holding a woman, a beautiful young woman whose lips were warm and sweet, whose breasts were flattened against his chest, whose soft belly was pressed to his. He'd known women before. After all, he had been married for a long time. When he had finished mourning for his beloved wife, he'd had no desire to marry again, but there had been a few visits to soiled doves when he went down to Sherman to pick up supplies for the stage station. He was fully aware of what he was doing, all right.

But it had never been like this before, not even with his wife.

The only problem was that the girl happened to be married to his son.

Maxwell tore his mouth away from Sandra's and said, "Oh, damn. Damn, damn, damn . . ." The cursing trailed off into a heartfelt whisper.

"It's all right, Jake," she said.

"No, it's not! You're my . . ."

"I know who I am," she interrupted. "And I know who you are. And I don't care, not now." She lifted her face to his and kissed him again.

The fingers of Maxwell's big hands splayed out against her back. He knew he shouldn't be doing this, knew it was all wrong and against every moral code there was. But he couldn't help himself. If Sandra had screamed or slapped him, he could have slunk away like some cur, but instead she seemed more than happy to be there in his arms, her mouth hot and urgent under his.

Hell, she wanted this as much as he did!

That realization burst on him with stunning force. All along, her reactions to his lustful glances had puzzled him. Now it was clear she felt the same way. Maxwell didn't know what to make of that, but he could ponder on it later.

Right now he had better things to do.

When they broke the second kiss, Sandra rested her head against his shoulder. He lifted a hand and stroked her hair, breathing deeply of the sweet scent coming from it. Her breath was warm against his throat. After a few moments, she asked in a whisper, "What are we going to do?"

That same question had begun to echo in Maxwell's brain. What *could* they do? It was bad enough they'd wound up hugging and kissing like this.

They certainly couldn't let this go any farther. For one thing, Theodore might come walking in at any moment and catch them.

Maxwell felt a flush of shame. He told himself he ought to be worried about lusting after his daughter-in-law, rather than thinking about being caught in the act. This was the worst thing he had ever done.

If only it hadn't felt so damned good, he thought.

He took a deep breath and said, "This has to be the end of it, Sandy. You and me both know this ain't right, and it can't go on." He thought she was about to say something in protest, so he hurried on, "I'm mighty sorry things ain't worked out for you and Ted like we all hoped they would. But it won't make things any better for you and me to . . . to . . ."

"Sin together?" Her voice sounded faintly mocking as she spoke without looking up at him.

"Well, dammit, that's what it'd be! You know it is."

"I never realized you were that much of a churchgoer, Jake."

"Never cared for sittin' on a hard pew 'til my rear end went numb whilst some sky pilot stood up front and hollered for a few hours. That's torture, not worshippin'. But I still recollect what's right and wrong, Sandy, and this . . . thing . . . between us is wrong."

She slipped out of his arms and turned away, and even though that was what he wanted, he still felt a sharp pang of regret that he was no longer holding her. "I know it," she said without looking at him. "It . . . it just felt so wonderful to be held by a decent man again, a man who cares about me. . . ."

"Of course I care about you." He made his voice firm as he reminded them both, "After all, you're my daughter-in-law."

"Yes. I am." She sighed heavily. "I guess you'd better go, Jake."

"Reckon so." He went to the doorway, paused, and looked back at her, hoping he wasn't making the biggest mistake of his life. "Good night, Sandy. Will you be all right?"

"Sure," she answered with a short, humorless laugh. "I'll be just fine."

Maxwell wished he could believe her.

But he didn't wait to debate the matter. Instead, he walked to the stage station as fast as his long legs would carry him.

A figure emerged from the trees nearby, a few minutes after Jake Maxwell had returned to the stagecoach station. The man stood there, his eyes staring stonily at the station building for a long moment before they swung over to the trading post. The store, like the station, was brightly lit. He generally kept the trading post open late for any customers who couldn't come by during the day. Sometimes travelers stopped at night, too.

Theodore Maxwell's lips compressed into a thin line. He had no idea why his father had been inside the trading post for such a long time. He wasn't close enough to have seen what was going on through the open door. But whatever was going on, he knew he didn't like it. Sandra and the old man were getting much too friendly. She was liable to start talking to his father about her husband's frequent absences. She was a bitch with a suspicious mind. There was no telling what she had figured out.

He had to put a stop to that growing friendship. Now, with everything he had ever wanted almost in his grasp, he couldn't take any chances.

Even if it meant that the old man had to die.

Chapter Six

The wound in Nacho's side felt much better the next morning. He was able to climb out of bed with only faint twinges of pain from the muscles around the injury. When Billy Cambridge changed the dressing after breakfast, the redness around the wound was nearly gone.

"No sign of infection." Cambridge nodded approvingly. "If you're careful, that wound ought to heal just fine, Nacho."

"That means I can ride a horse again, and we can start hunting down those outlaws," Nacho said with a grin.

"Not so fast. I didn't say anything of the sort."

"But you didn't say I couldn't ride," Nacho pointed out. "You know I'm always careful on horseback, Billy. It's not like I'm going to be riding Diablo or anything like that."

Jake Maxwell was sitting at the table in the station's big main room, thumbing tobacco from a rawhide pouch into his pipe. "Diablo," he repeated. "Mighty nasty-soundin' critter."

Nacho's grin widened. "He is. The biggest, blackest, meanest horse you've ever seen. But he can run like the wind when he's in the mood."

"Nacho's ridden Diablo in a dozen or more horse races around Pecos," Cambridge said as he began to wind some fresh strips of bandage around the foreman's torso, just as a precaution.

"And we've never been beaten yet," Nacho added proudly.

Dryly, Cambridge asked, "What about that time he acted up in the starting gate and threw you? Tried to stomp a hole clean through you, didn't he?"

Nacho shrugged. "I always figured that time didn't count, Billy. After all, we never got out of the gate. You can't say we lost, because we never ran."

"But you didn't win."

"But we didn't *lose*," Nacho insisted. "Being scratched from the field because some devil horse is jumping up and down on your head isn't the same. Is it?"

Cambridge shook his head and put the finishing touches on the bandage. "I won't argue the matter with you," he said. He gestured toward the table and went on, "Sit down and finish your coffee. Then we'll talk about trying to pick up the trail of those bandits."

Nacho's grin widened as he put on his shirt and settled down on the bench to finish his coffee. Cambridge went around the table and sat down on the other side, across from Maxwell.

"You remember what we talked about yesterday, Billy," the stationmaster said, "if you start out after that gang today."

"I will," Cambridge promised.

Nacho looked back and forth between them. "What did I miss?" he asked.

"Jake just helped refresh my memory about the lay of the land," Cambridge replied, draining the rest of the strong black brew in his own cup. "And we discussed the fact that you and I can't hope to capture those men by ourselves, Nacho."

"We can't? Why not? There were only six of them," Nacho said in complete seriousness.

"That we know of. There could have easily been more of them waiting back wherever they hide out. Anyway, three to one odds is a little higher than I like."

"But you told me that when you rode across the Rio Bravo with *Señor* Maxwell here and Prescott and Rip Ford and the other Rangers, there were only fifty of you against a thousand Mexican renegades. Those odds were much higher, and yet you prevailed."

"Well . . ."—Cambridge grimaced—"that was different."

Maxwell had broken into a broad grin. "And Billy might've exaggerated just a mite, Nacho."

"Besides, we were all a lot younger then," Cambridge said. "Remember, Nacho, I'm the lawyer. It's my job to turn folks' words around."

"Sí, I forgot." Nacho stood up. "I'm ready to ride."

"So am I," Cambridge said thankfully. "Just remember what we were talking about. All we want to do is locate the gang's hide-out. Then we'll let the authorities take care of them."

"Sure," Nacho said with a sigh. "That's fine, Billy."

Ten minutes later, they were saddled up and ready to leave. Cambridge was riding the same horse he had borrowed from Maxwell the day before, and Nacho was atop a rangy, mouse-colored, lineback dun. "He's not much to look at," Maxwell told Nacho, "but he's got sand."

"I can tell," Nacho agreed. "Thanks for letting me ride him, Jake."

"Just don't let those owlhoots get hold of him. They're probably horse thieves, too."

Nacho promised, "I'll bring him back safe and sound."

The two men rode away from the station, heading straight back down the road that would bring them to the spot where the stagecoach had been held up. Cambridge set the pace and kept it slow. Nacho knew perfectly well why the lawyer was being so leisurely about things. Billy was trying to take it easy on him, and that knowledge grated on Nacho. He had never been one to ask favors, and he hated to start now.

A little after mid-morning, they reached their destination. Cambridge reined in and pointed out the tracks to Nacho.

Looking around the scene, Nacho felt a slight chill go through him. This was the spot where he had been gunned down and had come awfully close to death. Solemnly, he looked at the road where his body had been sprawled after the leader of the gang shot him.

"Billy," he said quietly, "I really want to catch up to them. I don't want them to get away with this."

"Neither do I," Cambridge replied. "You think you can follow those tracks?"

Nacho nodded grimly. "I can follow them."

They edged their horses off the road and headed across the open range. Along the road, the terrain was mostly gently rolling, wooded hills and grassy fields, but both men knew it wouldn't be long until they reached more rugged country.

A full canteen hung from each saddlehorn, and the saddlebags contained enough biscuits and jerky for their noon meal. The fare was as plain as it could be, but it would keep them going. Cambridge planned to return to the Red River station that night so that Nacho could rest in a bunk at least one more time. Later on, if need be, they would bring more supplies and stay out three days or five days or however long it took to find the outlaws. Today's trip, though, was more of a feeler than anything else.

Nacho kept his keen eyes on the ground as they rode, letting Cambridge watch their back trail and the area around them. The tracks left by the outlaws were very faint at times—a stone scarred by the shoe of a passing horse, a broken branch on a bush, a strand of horsehair snagged by a bramble. There were other stretches of ground where the trail was as plain as day. Regardless, Nacho followed the signs with little trouble.

By noon the two men had covered several miles. The only problems they had encountered so far had occurred when the trail crossed a couple of small creeks. Nacho had been forced to search up and down the banks for the spot where the outlaws had emerged from the streams. Each time, though, they had picked up the tracks after only a short delay.

Cambridge called a halt when the sun was directly overhead. "Let's have some lunch," he suggested. "You need rest and food if you're going to get your strength back."

Nacho looked offended. "I'm fine," he declared. "A ride like this is nothing. I could do it with a dozen gunshot wounds."

"Well, let's just worry about the one you've already got, all right?"

Nacho snorted in disgust as he swung down from his horse, but when his booted feet hit the ground, he had to clutch the saddlehorn for a second while a wave of dizziness washed over him. It passed quickly, and he hoped that Cambridge hadn't noticed that something was bothering him. Billy was enough of a mother hen already, Nacho thought.

But if the truth had been told, he was a little tired. It would feel good to sit down under a tree, eat some biscuits and gnaw a strip of jerky, and drink some of the water from his canteen. If the circumstances had been different, he might have even lowered his head and tilted his Stetson down over his eyes for a little nap. They couldn't afford that luxury, though, not with a band of outlaws to catch.

As if reading his mind, Cambridge asked, "How are you really feeling, Nacho?"

"I told you, I'm fine," the *vaquero* insisted.

"You're looking a little pale."

Nacho took his canteen and the cloth sack full of provisions from his saddlebag and settled down cross-legged on the ground with his back against the trunk of an oak tree. He said, "If I'm pale, it is because you try to keep me cooped up so that I never see the sun. Quit worrying about me, Billy. Think about those desperados we're chasing instead."

"Maybe you're right," Cambridge said as he sat beneath another tree with his lunch. He tore off a hunk of biscuit, munched on it for a moment, then washed it down with a swig of water from his canteen. "This is a far cry from the meal I had yesterday over at the Baptist church. You should have seen it, Nacho." The attorney launched into a description of all the food that had been available.

Nacho listened for a few moments, then looked down at his biscuit and jerky and let out a groan. "Stop torturing me, Billy," he pleaded. "Next Wednesday you have to take me with you. I could do with a little religion."

"I won't disagree with that. But I hope we've got that money back and are long gone by next Wednesday."

For a few minutes, they ate in silence, the only sounds coming from birds and small animals in the brush. Suddenly, Nacho looked up, his jaw freezing in mid-chew as he concentrated on the unexplained noise he had just heard. It had sounded like a small rock bouncing down a slope.

And something about it, some inexplicable sensation, told him the noise hadn't been made by an animal.

A man had accidentally kicked that rock.

Nacho resumed gnawing the jerky. Around a mouthful of the stuff, he said without looking at Cambridge, "Keep eating, Billy. We got company."

Cambridge's flicker of reaction lasted only a split-second and was almost unnoticable. He said quietly, "You sure about that?"

"Pretty sure. Reckon there's somebody on that brushy hill over there to your right."

Cambridge looked out the corner of his eye at the slope some thirty yards away. "I don't see anything."

"Neither do I. But I heard something."

Cambridge gave a miniscule nod, knowing how sharp Nacho's hearing was. "Think somebody's trying to bushwhack us?"

"Don't know." Nacho reached down to shift his canteen on the ground beside him, but in actuality he was putting his hand only a couple of inches from the butt of his new Colt. "I'm watching for sunlight on a gun barrel. . . ."

Even as he spoke, he saw a bright glint on the hillside.

"Spread out!" he cried, palming out his pistol as he threw himself down and rolled away from Cambridge. The lawyer reacted instantly, moving in the opposite direction. Nacho wound up behind the trunk of another tree, and a quick glance told him that Cambridge had sought out the same type of shelter. Lining his gunsight on the hill, Nacho waited for shots to break out.

The shots didn't come, but he did see the brush on the side of the hill begin to wave as someone scurried through it. He could hear the rapid flight of footsteps from whoever had been spying on them, too. The unseen observer was heading for the top of the slope in a hurry.

"He's getting away, Billy!" Nacho called. "We've got to go after him."

"What if it's a trap?"

"What if it's one of those outlaws?" Nacho countered. "We don't want the whole bunch knowing we're out here looking for them!"

"You're right," Cambridge said grimly, coming to his feet. "Let's get mounted."

With his skin crawling a little from the knowledge that there could be other ambushers lurking nearby, Nacho came out into the open and ran over to his horse, scooping up the canteen and food along the way. He and Cambridge hit the saddle within seconds of each other, and they turned their horses toward the hill, urging the animals into a run.

As they started up the slope, Nacho caught a glimpse of a man topping the hill. All he saw was a floppy-brimmed hat with an eagle feather stuck into the band, but that was enough. Their quarry disappeared over the crest as Nacho and Cambridge sent the horses up the rugged hill.

They had not quite made it to the top when the sound of hoofbeats reached their ears. "He got to his horse!" Nacho called. He dug his heels into the flanks of the dun, trying to get more speed out of the animal. Cambridge was just behind him and to the right.

Nacho's mount went sailing over the top of the hill, its hooves clattering on the rocky ground as it struggled to maintain its balance. The slope on the other side was more gradual, falling away into a valley with another creek winding through it. Nacho saw a buckskin-clad man on a big bay vanishing into the trees along the stream.

Cambridge spotted him, too, and shouted to Nacho, "That's not one of the outlaws! None of them were wearing buckskins or a feather in their hat!"

"Could be another member of the gang! You said there might be more of them!" Nacho replied, using Cambridge's earlier logic. He holstered his gun but didn't slow down.

Neither did Cambridge, and Nacho knew the lawyer agreed with him. They had to catch up to the man on the bay. Even though he hadn't fired at them, they had to know who he was and why he had been watching them from hiding.

Obviously, the man they were chasing knew this territory. He rode confidently, ducking through openings in the brush, avoiding gullies, and taking shortcuts that led him around the roughest of the terrain. But Nacho and Cambridge stuck to him stubbornly, sometimes falling back a little, then regaining lost ground. Nacho had a feeling that both his horse and Cambridge's had more speed than the other man's mount, but that didn't count for much in a pursuit like this. Quickness, stamina, and responsiveness to a rider's commands were much more vital than sheer running ability.

Nacho felt pain pluck at his side. So far, the hectic ride hadn't caused his wound to open up again, but the constant pounding and jerking couldn't be good for it. He wasn't going to slow down and back off, though. The buckskin-clad man might prove to be important in locating the bandits who had held up the stagecoach.

A half-hour passed, and they weren't any closer to the other man than when they had started. He still had a lead of several hundred yards. The blood was roaring in Nacho's head, and he knew he would have to stop soon. He hoped that he and Cambridge could find their way out of here; he had been too busy chasing the man in buckskins to pay too much attention to the landmarks they were passing. Still, they knew they were west of the road between Sherman and the Red River station. All they had to do was head east, and they would hit the trail sooner or later.

He wasn't going to assume defeat that easily, Nacho told himself. He leaned forward in the saddle, grimacing as the motion pulled against the tightly wrapped bandages around his torso. Urging his horse on, he tightened his grip on the reins.

The man on the bay rode over the top of another hill, momentarily dropping out of sight. Nacho and Cambridge rode hard after him, and when they galloped over the rise a couple of minutes later, they fully expected to see him again.

But he was nowhere in sight.

Nacho reined in and stared. A grassy field, beginning to turn brown with the onset of fall, spread out in front of them. The meadow was at least five hundred yards wide. A thick stand of trees grew on the other side of the open space, but the buckskin-clad man hadn't had time to reach them.

"What the devil!" Cambridge exclaimed, coming to a stop beside Nacho.

To their left was more open ground, three hundred yards of it before some brush sprang up. In the other direction, to their right, was a thin line of trees. The rider they were pursuing might have had time to reach those trees, but the growth was so sparse that they should have still been able to see him.

"Where did he go?" Nacho asked, staring in disbelief. "He could not just disappear. . . ."

"Looks like that's what he did, amigo," Cambridge said. "Listen close. Do you hear hoofbeats?"

Nacho squinted and tilted his head to the side in concentration. After a long moment, he was forced to admit that he couldn't detect any sounds of flight.

"This makes no sense, Billy. A man doesn't just vanish, and neither does a horse."

"You're right. But where did he go?"

His eyes narrowing even more, Nacho studied the trees to their right. "A man might be able to hide behind one of those trunks," he mused. "If he could get his horse to lie down in the tall grass, we might not be able to see it."

Cambridge nodded slowly. "It's a cinch he didn't go either of the other directions. You think he's trying to set up another ambush?"

"I figure on finding out," Nacho said as he heeled his horse into a walk. He pointed its nose toward the trees.

"We could be riding right into a trap," Cambridge pointed out. He fell in alongside Nacho as they rode slowly and deliberately toward the grove of young, slender oaks. The lawyer's forehead was wrinkled in thought. "You know, I thought somebody was spying on me yesterday when I first checked out those tracks on the road. It could be this is the same person."

"Either way, whoever this is had chances to bushwhack us and didn't," Nacho said. "I'm curious, Billy. Who'd want to be keeping track of what we're doing?"

Cambridge hazarded a guess. "The outlaws, maybe?"

That made sense, Nacho thought. The gang probably thought this part of the country was their private stomping grounds; they'd be mighty interested in anybody who came poking around.

Nacho was watching the trees closely as he and Cambridge approached. The tension had made him forget all about the ache in his side from the bullet graze. This was no time to think about anything except avoiding the potential ambush.

No shots rang out as they neared the trees, and Nacho couldn't detect anyone lurking behind the trunks. He and Cambridge drew their guns as they rode into the oaks and looked around.

"He's not here," Cambridge grunted as he glanced around in puzzlement. "Where the hell did he go?"

On the other side of the trees, the landscape opened up into another pasture. If the man on the bay had ridden straight through the trees and kept going, he would have still been in sight.

Nacho studied the field closely, then abruptly said, "There's something funny out there, Billy." He lifted the hand holding the reins and pointed.

Cambridge shook his head. "I don't see anything. It just looks like an open field to me."

"Come on." Nacho walked his horse into the tall grass. Cambridge followed closely behind him.

They had ridden about thirty yards into the meadow when Nacho halted again. He nodded to the narrow gully that cut across the clearing in front of them. "That's where the man went," Nacho declared.

Cambridge studied the gash in the earth. The grass was nearly a yard high on both banks, and the gully was so narrow, only five feet across, that it was almost invisible only a few paces away. The banks were steep for the most part, but there were places where they had crumbled away enough for a man to lead a horse down into the wash.

Nacho leaned over in the saddle and pointed to tracks on the dusty floor of the gully. "Those are fresh. You can see both the hoofprints and the tracks left by that hombre's boots as he led the horse away. That's why we didn't hear anything. He slipped away slow and quiet. I told you he knows this country, Billy. He had to know this gully was here. It's not the sort of thing you stumble on by accident."

"He knows where he's going, all right," Cambridge agreed. "He just didn't count on you having such sharp eyes. Let's go."

They rode down into the wash, letting the horses pick their own way. It was a simple matter to follow the tracks left by the man in buckskins; he hadn't tried to conceal his trail, no doubt thinking that his pursuers would be thrown off the scent by this partially hidden escape route.

The gully zigged and zagged back toward the thickest growth of trees, gradually deepening until it was a good-sized cut in the earth. The banks were taller than the heads of Nacho and Cambridge as they rode along the wash. Twenty minutes after finding the gully, the two men reached a rocky bluff. The gully sloped down sharply, but their horses were able to negotiate the gravely path. They found themselves at the bottom of the bluff, looking out at another valley.

The first thing Nacho noticed was the tendril of smoke climbing into the sky. Cambridge saw it, too, and said, "Somebody's campfire. Maybe the man we're chasing."

Nacho shook his head. "No, it's coming from a chimney. See, there's a cabin over there in those cottonwoods along that creek."

Cambridge looked again and nodded after a moment. "You're right. I guess my eyes are going in my old age."

"Don't feel bad, Billy. You weren't supposed to see it."

Indeed, the log cabin was build right among the cottonwoods and blended in with its background. The only thing that stood out was the rock chimney, and it didn't extend very far above the level of the cabin roof.

"You see that bay horse anywhere?" Cambridge asked.

"Nope, but it could be tied up on the other side of the cabin. We can't just ride up there in the open, Billy."

"We sure as hell can't. That'd be asking to get shot. We'll circle around, come in from behind and keep an eye on the place for a while."

Nacho nodded in agreement with the attorney's plan and turned his horse to the left. They veered wide of the cabin. This maneuver might not fool whoever was in there, but at least they would have a chance.

They took their time approaching the building, slipping down from their horses and covering the last stretch on foot. There was a good chance this was the hide-out of the bandits who had robbed the stagecoach, Nacho knew, so he and Cambridge couldn't go busting in there. That would just get them killed. They had to keep an eye on the cabin until they could be sure who was inside, then they could ride for help.

Settling down behind some brush about a hundred feet from the cabin, they studied the scene eagerly. There was still no sign of the bay horse had been following, but now they could see a big lean-to behind the cabin. Several mounts could be concealed there.

"No way of knowing how many men are in there," Cambridge whispered. "We may have to wait a long time."

"I'm in no hurry," Nacho replied. He stretched out on his belly, hoping there weren't too many fleas and chiggers and ticks around here, and fastened his gaze on the log cabin. The building looked old, but it wasn't run down at all. Somebody took good care of it.

They had been lying there watching the cabin for less than ten minutes when something touched Nacho on the neck. Thinking it was a flea, he started to reach up to brush it away. That was when a hard ring of metal pressed into his flesh.

"Don't move, either one of you, or I'll blow this man's head off."

Nacho stiffened in shock, and his surprise wasn't entirely due to the fact that somebody had been able to sneak up on him.

The voice was female.

Chapter Seven

Cambridge was lying just as still as Nacho. Without moving his head, he said, "Just take it easy, whoever you are. We don't mean any harm."

"Sure," the girl said sarcastically. "Two gun-hung gents come skulking around in the brush, but they don't mean any harm. Tell me another."

"It's true, *señorita*," Nacho insisted. He swallowed nervously. He liked to think he was as brave as most men, but there was something about having a gun barrel pressed against your neck . . . He went on hurriedly, "We were lost, and when we saw that cabin, we thought whoever lived there might be able to tell us how to get back to the main trail."

"Then why didn't you just ride up and ask for directions?"

Cambridge answered that question, picking up on Nacho's story. "This is a rough country, miss. We were trying to see who was around before we went barging in. Some folks get nervous and quick on the trigger whenever strangers come around."

"That's true enough, I suppose." The gun barrel went away from Nacho's neck, and he felt relief wash through him. "You can turn over and sit up. Just do it slow and easy, and keep your hands away from those guns."

From her voice, Nacho knew she was young, but the tone of easy command in her words told him she was experienced in the ways of the frontier. He wasn't prepared, however, for what he saw when he rolled over and sat up.

The girl probably wasn't quite out of her teens, and she was lovely. Long, straight hair the color of midnight hung down her back. Eyes almost as dark regarded the two men warily. A dress of soft buckskin clung to her slender figure. The Indian blood in her veins was obvious, but her features were those of a white girl. The only thing marring her beauty was a thin white scar that ran across her cheek from her nose nearly to her left ear.

"You!" Cambridge exclaimed in surprise.

The girl frowned, shifting slightly the muzzle of the Spencer carbine she held. "Do I know you?" she demanded.

"I saw you yesterday over at the Sand Ridge Baptist Church, while they were having their weekly dinner on the grounds," Cambridge replied. "You were, ah, dressed differently, but I'm sure it was you. I couldn't be mistaken about . . ."

"About this?" she broke in, tilting her head to bring the scar on her cheek into prominence. Her mouth tightened into a bitter line.

"I was going to say, I couldn't be mistaken about such an attractive young lady."

Nacho spoke up, trying to keep his tone light. "I'm the one who is supposed to tell the girls how pretty they are, remember, Billy?"

"Both of you shut up," the girl snapped. "I'm trying to figure out what to do with you."

"You could let us go," Nacho suggested, then abruptly fell silent as the muzzle of the Spencer centered on his forehead.

He glanced over at Cambridge and saw the frown on the lawyer's face. Cambridge had to be just as baffled by this unexpected development as he was. What connection, if any, did this girl have with the man they had been chasing? Did she live in the log cabin? Was she part of the outlaw band, kept by the owlhoots to cook and clean for them—and to satisfy their lust whenever they felt like it?

Those questions raced through Nacho's brain. Unfortunately, he didn't have an answer for any of them.

The girl backed away several steps, the barrel of the carbine never wavering as she did so. "I'm going to let the old man decide what to do with you," she said.

Nacho and Cambridge exchanged a quick look. What old man? Maybe the buckskin-clad hombre they had been chasing? That made sense.

"Put your guns on the ground and then stand up," the girl ordered. "And just so you don't get any ideas, you ought to know I've been shooting squirrels and rabbits since I was five years old. There's seven bullets in this repeater; that'd be plenty for both of you."

"You're a very dangerous young lady," Nacho said dryly, wanting to see how she would react to a little prodding. "Shooting squirrels is not like shooting men."

"You're right. Men are a lot bigger targets. Easier to hit."

Nacho shrugged and reached across his body to use his left hand to ease the Colt from its holster. He laid the gun on the ground beside him. Cambridge did likewise, and then both men climbed slowly to their feet.

"Now back off."

They did so, stopping when they were a dozen feet from the pistols. The girl darted forward, holding the Spencer with one hand while she scooped up the revolvers with the other. As she was bent over, Nacho looked at Cambridge again and saw the lawyer give a tiny shake of his head. They wouldn't try jumping her. They'd probably find out more, faster, by playing along.

The girl held the Colts by the trigger guards in her left hand and used the right to gesture with the barrel of the carbine. "You were so interested in the cabin. Now lift your arms and get moving toward it."

The two men walked out of the brush with the girl following behind them. They held their empty hands at shoulder height. Their path wound through the trees around the cabin, and as they drew nearer, the rear door of the building swung open.

A man stepped into view in the doorway, cradling a Winchester in his arms. He was hatless, but even without the feather-decorated headgear, Nacho recognized the buckskins of the man he and Cambridge had pursued for the last hour. The man's face was lined and leathery from a lifetime spent in the sun. His hair was still dark, but the short beard on his chin was mostly silver. As Nacho came closer, he saw that the man's shaggy hair had been twisted into two short braids, one lying on each shoulder. He studied Nacho and Cambridge with intent blue eyes as the girl marched them up to the cabin.

"What you caught there, Dove?" the man rasped.

"Stop," the girl told her captives. To the old man, she said, "They were snooping out there in the brush, Pa, just like we figured they'd be. City fellas, more than likely. They never heard me slipping around behind them."

"I am no . . . no tenderfoot!" Nacho declared angrily. "I am Ignacio Alexander Rodriguez Graves, and I am the best *vaquero* in all of West Texas!"

"West Texas is a long way off, boy," the man in buckskins said. "What are you doin' pokin' around this part of the country?"

Cambridge pointed out, "We could ask you the same question, sir. And in addition, we could ask you why *you* were spying on *us*."

The old-timer squinted suspiciously at the attorney. "You look like a cowhand who's seen better days, mister, but you talk like one of them lawyer fellas. Just who the hell are you?"

"My name is Billy Cambridge, and I'm an attorney, all right. My friend Nacho has already introduced himself. We seem to be at a disadvantage where you're concerned, however."

"You mean you want to know my name? What business is it of yours?"

Cambridge didn't answer right away, and neither did Nacho. The foreman's mind was working swiftly. He hadn't heard any other voices or sounds of movement from inside the cabin, and it was looking more likely that the old man and the girl were alone here. That didn't mean they weren't connected with the outlaws anyway, but somehow Nacho didn't think that was the case. Maybe he just didn't want to believe anything too bad of a girl as pretty as the one called Dove.

Cambridge finally spoke, his words revealing that he had come to the same conclusion as Nacho. "It's our business if your name is Seamus O'Shea," Cambridge said. "We have a mutual friend—Jake Maxwell."

The eyes of the buckskin-clad man widened. "Friends of Maxwell's are you?" he demanded. "You got any proof of that?"

"We're staying with him at the Red River stage station." Cambridge inclined his head toward the brush behind them. "The horses we're riding are tied up back there. They carry Maxwell's brand."

The old man snorted in derision. "You wouldn't be the first horse thieves to try to lie their way out of trouble with some fancy story."

"Dammit, I'm getting tired of this," Cambridge snapped. "Either you're O'Shea or you're not. If you are, you've got nothing to fear from us. If you're not, and if you're mixed up with a bunch of outlaws who are using this area as their headquarters, then you'd better just go ahead and shoot us. Or have your daughter do it. She seems quite capable of shooting two men in the back."

"Here now! You got no call to talk about my girl that way." The man glowered at them. "I'm Seamus O'Shea. Speak your piece." He glanced over their shoulders at the girl. "Dove, lower that carbine. But keep it handy."

"Yes, Pa," she said.

"Can we put our hands down now?" Cambridge asked O'Shea. The old man nodded curtly.

"Thanks," Nacho said as he lowered his arms. "I was getting tired. I got shot a couple of days ago, you know."

"How the hell would I know that? Don't try to trick me, boy. I seen and heard it all. I seen the elephant a dozen times 'fore you was even thought of."

Before Nacho could respond, Cambridge said, "I think we can settle this peacefully. A couple of days ago, Nacho and I were passengers on a northbound stagecoach that was stopped and held up by bandits. The outlaws wounded Nacho, knocked me out, and stole a great deal of money, money that I was delivering to a client. The stage went on, but we stayed to try to find those outlaws. They fled in this direction. I'm taking a chance and telling you the truth because Jake Maxwell is an old friend of mine from the days we were both Rangers, and he seems to think you're an honest man, O'Shea."

For a long moment, O'Shea didn't say anything. Finally, he grunted, "Come out here huntin' owlhoots, did you? Well, it's a good place for it. I hear tell there's a bunch around here somewheres, but I wouldn't know nothin' about 'em."

"Why were you watching us from that hill?" Nacho wanted to know.

"I was out huntin' and saw a couple of strangers." O'Shea rubbed his grizzled jaw. "Reckon I'm just naturally curious."

Cambridge said, "We saw sunlight reflecting off a gun barrel and thought somebody was about to ambush us."

O'Shea snorted again and tapped the pocket of his buckskin shirt. "You saw sunlight hittin' my spyglass, that's what you saw. If I'd been interested in bushwhackin' you, you wouldn't've knowed I was anywheres about until the bullet hit you."

"Why did you run when we spotted you?" Nacho asked.

"Hell, you went to divin' around and pullin' guns. For all I knew, you was a pair of road agents yourselves. All I knew for sure was that I didn't have any business with you, and I didn't see the point of hangin' around for a bunch of worthless palaver." O'Shea spat into the dirt beside the back door. "'Course, that's what I wound up gettin' anyway."

"All right, we've all told our stories," Cambridge said. "I think it's time to call a truce and put away the guns. Jake thought maybe you could help us."

O'Shea shook his head. "Jake thought wrong. I already told you I don't know nothin' about any outlaws. If you want to keep pokin' around these woods, that's your own look-out. Don't strike me as a real sensible thing to do, but I ain't never been one to tell another fella how to live his life. Long as you don't bother us, we won't bother you."

"Pa!" the girl exclaimed. "You don't believe them, do you? After the way they chased you?"

"The yarn they tell makes sense, Dove," O'Shea replied. "They look just dumb enough to be chasin' owlhoots through these breaks."

Nacho was about to frame a resentful retort when Cambridge shot him a warning look. The lawyer said, "We could do with a cup of hot coffee before we go."

"I'm sure you could," O'Shea shot back, "but I ain't offerin'. I want both of you to git."

Cambridge shrugged and nodded. "Let's go, Nacho." As he turned around, he said to Dove, "We'd like our guns back now, please."

"Mighty polite, aren't you?" the girl asked scornfully. She lowered the butt of the Spencer to the ground and leaned the carbine against her hip. With practiced ease, she thumbed the cartridges out of both Colts, then handed them over. As she dropped the bullets into each man's outstretched palm, she said, "Don't try to reload until you're a long way from here. I may be watching, and if I see you putting shells back in those guns, I'll shoot you out of the saddle."

Nacho slid his Colt back into its holster and put the cartridges into the pocket of his *charro* jacket. He looked over at Seamus O'Shea and said, "Your daughter, she is one tough *señorita*."

"Damn right," the old-timer growled. "Ain't nobody can say I don't know how to bring up a young'un."

Nacho and Cambridge exchanged a look, then walked back into the brush under the watchful eyes of O'Shea and Dove. They went to their horses, untied the animals, and mounted up. "What now, Billy?" Nacho asked.

"I think we've done enough for one day," Cambridge replied. "Let's go back to Jake's."

The two men rode in silence for the most part, each of them thinking their own thoughts about what had happened since they had left the stage station that morning. They followed the gully back to the spot where they had first found it, then gradually retraced the path they had taken while pursuing Seamus O'Shea. A few times, they were unsure which turn to take, but Nacho's dependable instincts when it came to directions continued to be correct. Just past the middle of the afternoon, they reached the place where they had stopped for lunch.

"I can pick up the tracks of those outlaws again," Nacho offered.

Cambridge shook his head. "It's too late in the day. We'll be doing good to get back to Jake's before nightfall. If you're able, we'll come back here tomorrow and bring more supplies next time."

"I'll be able," Nacho promised. "I still want to find those no-good crooks." He hesitated, then added, "Unless we already did."

"You mean O'Shea?" Cambridge asked. He looked a little relieved that one of them had finally brought up the subject. "What did you think of the old man's story?"

"I do not know, Billy," Nacho answered honestly. "I think he may have been telling the truth about not trying to ambush us. But I think a man like that would know what was going on around him. If there are outlaws operating in these parts—and we know there are—I think O'Shea would probably know where their hide-out is."

"I agree. Even if he doesn't have any connection with the gang, he knows more than he told us." Cambridge shrugged. "But we couldn't very well force him to reveal anything more than he chose to. Not under the circumstances."

"Not with that girl pointing a rifle at our backs, you mean." Nacho grinned. "She was quite a spitfire, eh?"

"That's for sure. I'm a little surprised she didn't just shoot us and not bother the old man with it." Cambridge looked suspiciously over at Nacho as they walked their horses along the trail. "I've heard that tone in your voice before, Nacho. You're not getting sweet on her, are you?"

"She was very beautiful," Nacho mused. "Even that scar just made the rest of her seem more elegant."

Cambridge laughed shortly. "He mother was probably a Comanche squaw, Nacho, and she's just about as civilized as a Comanche—not much!" He paused and scowled in thought. "At least that's the way she seemed today. But I suppose I could be jumping to a conclusion. She seemed perfectly respectable when I saw her at the church yesterday."

"She never did say what she was doing there."

"Maybe she's a member of the congregation. I can check with Reverend Livingston." Cambridge pushed back his hat. "To tell you the truth, I'm not sure what to make of Miss Dove O'Shea."

"I know one thing: I would like to see her again." Nacho added fervently. "The next time without a gun in her hand!"

As Cambridge had predicted, it was almost dark before they reached the Red River station. A band of crimson stretched along the western horizon, marking the spot where the sun had disappeared earlier. As they rode into the yard in front of the station, Jake Maxwell opened the door and stepped outside to greet them.

"I was wonderin' when you boys would get back," he said. "Have any trouble?"

"A little," Cambridge replied as he swung down from the saddle. "We ran into your friend Seamus O'Shea."

Maxwell grinned and reached for his pipe. "The old fella didn't try to part your hair with a bullet, did he? I should have warned you he can be a little touchy sometimes, until he gets to know you."

Nacho had dismounted and began loosening the saddle on his horse. "That warning is a little late, Jake," he said. "O'Shea didn't take a shot at us, but that daughter of his poked a rifle barrel in the back of my neck. It didn't make me feel too good."

The stationmaster looked more serious as he nodded and said, "So you met Dove. I didn't know whether she'd be around or not. She's sort of like the wind, comes and goes as she pleases. It's the Indian blood in her, I reckon. She can't stand to be cooped up in one place for too long."

"We'd like to hear more about her and O'Shea both," Cambridge said.

"Well, come on inside. I kept the stew and the coffee warm. You boys settle down to a surroundin' and I'll tell you about Seamus."

Nacho and Cambridge took their horses to the barn behind the station building, unsaddled and rubbed down the animals, then went inside to take Maxwell up on the offer. As Nacho stepped into the station, he breathed deeply of the blended aromas of stew and coffee and smiled. He felt better already.

When they were seated at the table with the food and drink in front of them, Maxwell fired up his pipe and began, "You could probably tell that O'Shea is an old frontiersman. He doesn't talk a lot about himself, but from what little he's said and what I've heard about him from other folks, I figure he was one of the first white men west of the Brazos. And he's damn sure one of the few white men who ever got along with the Comanch'."

"The girl is half-Comanche, isn't she?" Cambridge asked.

Maxwell nodded. "Dove's mama was the daughter of a Comanche war chief. The Indians didn't think too kindly of her when she got herself married to O'Shea. They made both of 'em leave, although O'Shea was welcome to come back for a visit now and then as long as he didn't bring his wife along. He made his livin' tradin' amongst the tribes."

"He was a Comanchero?" Nacho breathed, recalling tales of those hated white and Mexican renegades who had supplied the Comanches with guns to raid the Texas ranchers.

"Not then," Maxwell replied with a shake of his head. He puffed on the pipe for a moment, then resumed, "The Army wanted him to scout for them when they started tryin' to break the hold the Indians had on the frontier. But O'Shea wouldn't work against his wife's people, even though they'd made her leave. Reckon he wanted to do his best not to take sides. He was a white man, but he had a Comanche wife and a daughter by that time. Then some of those soldier boys got the idea O'Shea was betrayin' his own race by not helpin' them hunt down the Comanch'." Maxwell sighed heavily.

Nacho leaned forward eagerly, caught up in the story, his supper momentarily forgotten. "What happened?"

"O'Shea had a little spread not far from Fort Griffin. The commandin' officer called him to the fort one day and asked him again to sign on as a civilian scout. O'Shea turned him down flat, just like all the other times, and rode back home. But a handful of those troopers had overheard what O'Shea said to the colonel, and they followed him. Busted in on O'Shea and his wife and the little girl. Now, Seamus O'Shea is a pure-dee wildcat when it comes to fightin', or so I've heard, but he was outnumbered. Those soldiers beat the hell out of him and then molested his wife. The little girl tried to stop 'em, and one of the bastards took a swipe at her with his knife." Maxwell lifted his hand to his left cheek. "That's how she got that scar across her face. Laid her open to the bone. When the soldiers got through, they left O'Shea's wife there with him and the little girl. O'Shea was all busted up inside from the beatin' they gave him, and Dove had blood all over her face. Her mama thought they was both dead. She got O'Shea's Bowie and cut herself up, like those Indian women'll do when they're grievin'. 'Course, O'Shea wasn't dead, and neither was the girl. But Dove's mama sure was when she got through cuttin'."

Silence fell over the big room as Maxwell concluded his story. For long seconds that seemed even more stretched out than they really were, neither Nacho or Cambridge said anything. Then, finally, the lawyer asked, "Is that story really true, Jake?"

Maxwell shrugged. "Bits and pieces of it I got from Seamus himself, but most of the details come from other folks who lived around Fort Griffin at the time." He puffed on the pipe again and blew a cloud of gray smoke toward the ceiling. "That ain't all of it, though."

"What about the Comancheros?" Nacho asked.

"That's the part I was just comin' to. O'Shea was hit pretty damn hard by everything that happened, as you can imagine, and there's some say he went a little crazy for a while. But he was sane enough to take that girl to the fort and get the Army doctor to patch up her face. Made sure the sawbones did a good job of it, too—stood over him with a Henry rifle while he was sewin' up the cut. Then he left Dove with the preacher's family there in the town next to the Army post and took off. Next anybody heard of him, he was ridin' with a band of Comancheros in the Staked Plains. I figure what those soldiers did made him turn his back on the white man's world completely for a while. Seamus stayed with the Comancheros for a couple of years, then Mackenzie caught ol' Chief Quanah up there at Palo Duro Canyon and put an end to most of the fightin'. With the Indian wars over for the most part, there wasn't any business for the Comancheros. Some of 'em lit out across the Rio Grande or went over to New Mexico Territory. O'Shea wound up back here, and somewhere along the line, Dove got back together with him."

Nacho frowned. "You're saying the man was an outlaw, that he rode with the Comancheros. Why hasn't he been arrested?"

"That was a long time ago—"

"Only ten years!"

"And just because there were rumors that O'Shea was a Comanchero, that don't prove nothin'."

"Jake's right, Nacho," Cambridge said. "The law would need solid evidence that O'Shea traded guns to the Indians, especially this long after the fact."

Nacho stood up and paced away from the table, his features twisted with conflicting emotions. "If O'Shea was an outlaw then," he said without turning around, "he could be an outlaw now."

"I suppose that's true," Maxwell admitted. "But nobody's ever accused Seamus of doin' anything wrong since he came to this part of the country. I reckon I know him as well as anybody hereabouts, and I think he just wants to be left alone."

Nacho took a deep breath. "Comanches raided my father's ranch many times when I was a boy. None of my family was killed, but some of our *vaqueros* died, and the savages stole our stock until my father finally gave up. I . . . I don't see how anyone could have traded with them."

"People have their own reasons for the way they live their lives, and those reasons don't have to make sense to us or anybody else," Cambridge said. "I've got to admit I'm a little more suspicious of O'Shea now that I've heard your story, though, Jake. He knows the country around here, and he strikes me as tough enough to ride herd on a gang of desperados."

Maxwell nodded slowly. "Seamus is tough enough, all right. But I still can't believe it of him."

Nacho turned to face the other two men again. "I think we should keep an eye on this O'Shea," he said harshly. "Maybe he will lead us to the men who stole that money."

"We'll see," Cambridge said noncommittally. "Right now, you need to finish your supper and get some rest."

Grudgingly, Nacho came back to the table, but the food was tasteless to him now. He had hated Comancheros for years, but he had never expected to run into a former member of that despised breed at this late date. He was more convinced than ever that O'Shea was tied in somehow with the outlaws who had held up the stagecoach. He felt righteous anger simmering inside him.

But somehow, the face of the beautiful girl called Dove kept getting in the way. . . .

Chapter Eight

The light burning in the farmhouse window was a warm yellow glow in the night. Asa Graham leaned forward in his saddle and nodded to the other men sitting their horses next to him. "Let's ride on down there," he said.

He was in his late thirties, a rangy, lantern-jawed man with long pale hair that hung below his flat-crowned hat. Like the other men, he wore a long duster, which was pushed back at the moment so that he could more easily reach the long-barreled Remington holstered on his hip.

One of Graham's companions asked, "What about the masks? You want us to put them on?"

Graham shook his head and smiled bleakly. "No need."

The others all knew what he meant, and if any of them didn't like the idea, they didn't say anything about it. Slowly, with Graham in the lead, they rode down the hill toward the isolated North Texas farm.

This raid wasn't a matter of money; they had plenty of greenbacks. The last stagecoach robbery alone had netted them more money than all of them put together had seen in their entire lives. Most of the cash was still back at the hide-out, safely cached. They could have ridden into a town and bought anything they wanted.

Graham said they were going to lie low for a while, though, and most of the time, nobody was willing to argue with Graham. The last man who'd tried had wound up with a knife in his belly. Graham knew the others were afraid of him, and he liked the feeling.

They were running a little low on food, but with any luck, they would be able to replenish their supplies at this farm. Besides, Graham thought, these sodbusters had settled too close to the hide-out. A man in his business didn't have any use for close neighbors.

A dog began barking as the riders reached the bottom of the hill and started toward the house. A moment later, a rectangle of light appeared as someone inside the clapboard structure opened the door. A figure was silhouetted in the doorway.

Damn dumb farmer, Graham thought. A man that stupid didn't deserve to live.

He had to give the sodbuster credit, though. When the man spotted nearly a dozen riders bulking up out of the shadows, he ducked back inside quickly and slammed the door. The light in the window vanished as the lantern was blown out.

Graham lifted a hand as he and the others rode into the place's small, dusty yard. "That's far enough, boys," he said quietly.

A voice came from one of the windows. "Damn right that's far enough. I've got you covered. Who are you, and what do you want?"

It was doubtful the farmer could tell much about his expression in the dim light from a quarter moon, but Graham put a friendly smile on his face anyway. "Howdy," he called. "Sorry to come bustin' in on you like this. We're lookin' to water our horses."

"Well's over there by the barn," the farmer replied. "You're welcome to use it. Just don't come any closer to the house."

"Sure, mister, whatever you want." Graham laughed shortly. "Hell, the way you're actin', you'd think we were the James gang and I was old Jesse, come back to life."

"This is a lonely country. A man can't take chances with his family."

"We'll be on our way in a few minutes," Graham called back, trying to sound reassuring.

He led the others over to the well. They dismounted and gathered around as one man began hauling up the bucket. In the cluster of men and horses, it was difficult to pick out individual figures in the darkness.

"Ed, you and Jack go through the barn and slip around behind the house. The two of you ought to be plenty to take that sodbuster once you get inside."

"Sure, Asa. Come on, Jack."

The exchange was whispered, and there was no way the farmer could have heard it over the stamping of the restless horses. The two men Graham had picked for the job vanished through the open door of the barn into the darkness within. In a matter of moments, Graham knew, they would be breaking into the house from the back and disposing of the wary farmer. It probably wouldn't take but one shot, he thought.

Two minutes later, a small war started inside the house.

Graham jerked around as guns began blasting, hot and heavy. "Get in there!",he barked, sliding his own pistol from its holster. The rest of the gang turned and ran toward the house. A couple of them triggered off some shots, adding to the noise and confusion.

Surging into the lead as the shooting died away, Graham lifted a booted foot and smashed it against the door. The panel flew open, slamming back against the wall. Graham went through in a low crouch, gun in hand. A lot of things could be said about him, but he was no coward.

Just an outlaw and a cold-blooded murderer.

The gunfire might have ceased, but the house was still noisy. A woman was screaming, a man cursed fervently in a choked voice, and somebody was grunting and groaning in pain. Graham put his back against the wall and lifted his pistol, hammering back as the other outlaws poured into the room.

"Somebody get a light in here!" Graham ordered, then shifted quickly to one side just in case somebody tried to loose a shot at the sound of his voice.

A second later, a lucifer flared into life as one of the outlaws snapped his thumbnail across its head. The man lifted the match, sending its bright, harsh glare across the room.

Graham saw Ed and Jack, the two men he had sent in here, sprawled on the floor in bloody, loose-limbed heaps. He'd seen enough death to know that both of them were done for. So was the farmer, who had been driven into a corner by the slugs that had turned his shirtfront into a red ruin. He was sitting down, propped up by the walls, legs splayed out in front of him. A Winchester lay on the floor between those legs.

On the other side of the room, near a door that probably led into the kitchen, lay a boy in his late teens, the side of his head shot away. His fingers were still loosely clenched around the butt of an old Dance Brothers .44 revolver. Another boy, a little younger than the first, was on the other side of the doorway, curled up in a ball, gunshot from the look and sound of it.

A woman was crouched next to the body of the farmer. The sobbing and wailing came from her. A girl about twelve was kneeling beside her, eyes wide and staring, her fingers plucking idly at her mother's sleeve.

In the far corner was another man, also sitting propped up against the wall. Both shoulders were bloody and bullet-smashed, but that didn't stop him from trying futilely to pick up the Colt he had dropped. He was the one cursing. Graham looked from him to the woman and saw the resemblance. They were probably brother and sister.

So, the house had contained the sodbuster, his wife, the brother-in-law, and the three youngsters. Ed and Jack had walked in on four males, all of them armed and willing to put up a fight. No wonder such hell had broken loose. The two outlaws had done good to do as much damage as they had before they went down.

The outlaw holding the match let out a curse and shook his fingers as the flame reached them. Darkness dropped down over the room again. Graham snapped, "Strike another light!"

Quickly, one of the gang complied, and the scene hadn't changed when the second match flared up. Graham spotted a lamp sitting on a small table. Miraculously, it hadn't been broken by a stray bullet during the melee. He ordered the man with the match to light the lamp, and a moment later, its bright glow filled the room.

"That's better," Graham said. "I'm good with a gun, but even I need a little light to shoot by." He turned to face the wounded man, who still couldn't make either arm work in his attempt to retrieve his pistol. Graham lined the Remington on his forehead and fired. The man's head bounced off the wall behind it as the slug drove through his brain.

That started the woman screaming again as she crouched beside her dead husband. Graham strode across the room and slapped her, hard, jerking her head around. She gasped once and then fell silent.

"We'll be takin' your food," Graham told her. "You got any whiskey around here?" When she didn't answer, he repeated the question in a harsher tone and lifted his hand again threateningly.

"In . . . in the kitchen!" she babbled. After a second, she choked out, "Why . . . why did you do this? Why did you have to kill them?"

Graham shrugged. "Don't reckon we had to," he said, although they all knew differently. "Your men started the shootin'. All we want is food and whiskey and any money you've got. You got any money?"

"Under the loose floorboard . . . in the kitchen." The woman looked over at her daughter and sobbed.

Graham could understand why. The girl's eyes were as empty as could be. All the shooting and killing had done something to her head.

"Better that way," Graham said quietly. "She won't know what's goin' on."

The woman looked up at him, horrified realization in her eyes. As bad as it had been so far, the ordeal wasn't over.

An hour later, they rode away from the farm with a fresh stock of supplies, two partially empty bottles of whiskey, and eight dollars. Behind them, flames began to climb toward the Texas sky, consuming the farmhouse and the dead within.

There had been nights in the past when Jake Maxwell had not been able to sleep, especially during the months following his wife's death. He had found himself staring up at the darkened ceiling of the room they had shared in the stage station, playing out in his mind the memories of his life with her, sometimes until gray light crept in with the dawn.

Tonight he wasn't remembering his wife. He was thinking about another woman altogether.

Sandra . . .

The night before, after he had taken her into his arms and kissed her, his sleep had been disturbed, too, but then it had been dreams that bothered him, sinful dreams he didn't even want to think about now. This was different. He was staring at the ceiling again, wide awake, wishing that there was some way Sandra could come to him again, even though that was the last thing either of them needed.

Because Maxwell was awake, he heard the slow, steady hoofbeats and the soft creak of wheels turning.

Somebody was driving a vehicle of some sort down the trail toward the station, he realized as he sat up in his bunk and listened to the sounds. There was no stage due tonight. Maxwell swung his feet to the floor, stood up, and went into the main room. From the window near the front door, he could see down the road to the south.

A buggy was rolling along the tree-shrouded trail. If it had been broad daylight, Maxwell probably would have been able to recognize the vehicle or the horse pulling it, but tonight he could barely make it out in the shadows. There was nothing distinctive about it; dozens of people in the area drove similar buggies. But the question remained—why would anybody be coming to the station at this time of night?

And the answer was simple, of course, Maxwell realized as he watched the little two-wheeled carriage swing past the station. It was heading for the trading post instead.

It was a little unusual for Theodore to have customers this late, but not unheard of. He generally stayed open well after dark, since the farmers and ranchers in the area sometimes worked on their spreads from dawn to dusk and didn't have a chance to buy supplies during the day, but Maxwell judged it was midnight or later now. At least it seemed like he had been tossing restlessly in his bunk for several hours.

Quietly, so as not to disturb Billy Cambridge and Nacho Graves—who had had a hard day, after all—Maxwell opened the door of the station and stepped outside. The buggy was just pulling up in front of the trading post. When it had come to a stop, a man stepped down from it and went to the front door. Maxwell couldn't tell anything about him other than that he seemed to be fairly tall and was wearing dark clothes and a hat. The man lifted his arm and Maxwell supposed he was rapping on the door, but if so he was striking the panel softly enough that Maxwell couldn't hear it.

Something about the situation struck Maxwell as so strange that he took a step back into the doorway, deeper in shadow but where he could still keep an eye on the trading post. After a moment he saw a dim glow through the front window of the store. Theodore was answering the summons, Maxwell supposed, and was carrying a candle to light his way through the merchandise-crowded room.

When the door of the trading post opened, Maxwell saw he was right. The circle of light cast by the candle revealed Theodore standing there, his hair rumpled, wearing a jacket over his nightshirt. In his other hand he clutched a handgun, just in case of trouble. The visitor stepped back quickly, as if the light bothered him. Theodore must have recognized him, because he lowered the pistol and quickly blew out the candle.

Maxwell frowned. What the devil was the boy up to? The visitor went back to the buggy now, and Theodore followed him. The man in the suit stepped up into the vehicle, and Theodore leaned close to it, evidently to carry on a low-voiced conversation.

Something was wrong. That feeling gnawed at Maxwell's insides and made him draw back even more into the shadows. If the man in the buggy had gone inside the trading post and emerged a few minutes later with a bag of supplies, Maxwell wouldn't have thought there was anything unusual about that except the lateness of the hour, and there could be all sorts of reasons for that. Likewise, the visitor wasn't just asking directions, either, as folks sometimes did when they stopped at the trading post. The conversation was going on too long for that, and Theodore wasn't waving his arms around and pointing like he did whenever he was telling somebody how to get to where they were going. No, Maxwell concluded, this encounter was just downright unsettling.

After about ten minutes, Theodore stepped away from the buggy. Maxwell saw him nod, or at least imagined he did. At this distance, in the dim light, it was hard to be sure. The man in the buggy flapped the reins and got the horse moving again. He pulled the animal's head around and turned the buggy, heading it back down the road. Maxwell quickly closed the door of the station before the vehicle passed, although he would have had a hard time explaining why he did so. It just seemed like the smart thing to do under the circumstances.

When enough time had passed for the buggy to get out of sight, Maxwell stepped outside again and peered toward the trading post. Theodore had gone back in. The front door was closed, and the building was dark.

He could ask the boy what was going on, Maxwell thought, but chances were he wouldn't get an answer. Theodore would probably just get mad and accuse his father of spying on him. And that would be true enough, Maxwell realized. He had been spying.

But if Theodore was up to something he shouldn't be, Maxwell wanted to know about it. Theodore could get himself into trouble if he wanted to, but he had no right to drag Sandra into whatever was going on.

Maxwell grimaced as he went back into his room. Funny how Sandra always figured in his thinking these days. Most men would have been worried about their sons getting in some sort of trouble, but not him. He was more concerned with how it would affect his daughter-in-law.

But was it his fault Theodore had always been cool toward him, he asked himself as he got back into bed. He and Theodore had never been close, and after the boy's mother died, the gap had just grown wider. He loved his son, he told himself—but that wasn't always enough.

Sleep didn't come any easier now. He was even more restless than before. His watch was lying on the small table next to his bunk, and its ticking seemed to fill the room. Maxwell reached over and picked it up, ran his fingers over the smooth face as if he could somehow sense the hour just by touching it. He was going to be weary from lack of sleep tomorrow, that was for sure.

Some time had passed since Theodore's conversation with the mysterious visitor, but Maxwell wasn't sure how much. He heard the soft tapping on the little window above his bunk, thinking at first that he was imagining it. Gradually, though, he realized that someone was actually knocking on the glass that had been freighted up from Dallas and fit into the opening that had originally been covered by oilcloth. Maxwell sat up sharply, his hand going to the rifle that lay on the floor next to the bunk. He didn't have much call to use it lately, but he kept the weapon there out of habit, a reminder of the days right after the War when he had established the trading post. There had still been plenty of badmen in the area then.

And it looked like those days might be coming back, he thought grimly as he stood up to one side of the window, being cautious just in case whoever was out there decided to throw a shot through the glass.

He saw moonlight shining on long blond hair and knew he was in no danger. No danger of being shot at, anyway.

Leaning closer to the window, he unlatched it and swung it open. "Sandra?" he hissed. "That you, girl? What are you doin' out there at this time of night?"

"I need to talk to you, Jake," she answered in a whisper. "Can I come in?"

Billy and Nacho were probably light sleepers, Maxwell thought. He didn't want to bother them—and he didn't particularly want them knowing that he was talking to Sandra in the middle of the night, either. He said, "I'll meet you out in the barn in a minute."

She nodded and disappeared.

Maxwell took a deep breath and reached for his pants. He had stepped outside in just his long johns before, but he couldn't talk to a female dressed like that, not even Sandra. *Especially* not Sandra.

When he had his pants on, he poked his feet into his boots, picked up the rifle again, and slipped out of the station. He probably wouldn't need the rifle, but you couldn't ever tell when you'd run into a bobcat prowling around. It was sort of late in the year for snakes to be out and about, too, but he'd seen them before even closer to winter.

Circling the building, he went to the barn. One of the doors was open a couple of inches, the gap marked by a thick line of blackness seeping from the shadowy interior. Maxwell pushed the door back a little more and eased through.

A hand touched his arm. "Jake?"

"I'm here, girl," he said, deliberately making his voice gruff. "What's wrong?"

"I'm starting to get scared. Theodore . . . There's something strange about him, Jake. . . ."

Maxwell could have told her that a long time ago. But he knew what she meant. Theodore's behavior was getting even more erratic lately. Maxwell had seen him coming and going at odd hours, and that took on added—although still unknown—significance in light of the visit earlier by the man in the buggy.

"You must've seen that fella, too," Maxwell said. Sandra's fingers were still resting on his forearm, just below the sleeve of the long johns. Her touch was warm and bothersome.

"The man who drove up in the buggy? I didn't know you had seen him."

His eyes were adjusting to the darkness now, and he could make her out a little better. Amazing how her hair shone, even in this gloom. She was wearing a light-colored nightdress of some sort, and he could see it, too. He said, "I was havin' trouble sleepin' and heard that buggy pull up. Figured it wouldn't hurt to take a look and see what was goin' on. Couldn't tell much, though. I just saw a fella in a dark suit. Ted came out and talked to him for a while. That's all I know."

"I don't know much more than that." Sandra paused, and he listened to her breathing as she put her thoughts in order. Then she went on, "The knocking woke me up. It was real soft, like whoever it was didn't want to wake up anybody else. Theodore heard it, of course. Maybe he was waiting for it, for all I know. But he got up right away and lit a candle. I asked him where he was going, and he said we must have a late customer. I told him we'd never had a customer that late before, and he said it was none of my business." She made a sound in her throat, a sound of sadness that made Maxwell's mouth tighten into a grim line. "Actually he said it was none of my Goddamned business. And then when I started to get out of bed anyway, he shoved me back down and told me to stay there if I knew what was good for me."

A few times, when Theodore was a boy, Maxwell had been forced to take a strap to him. He felt like doing the same thing right now.

"I waited until he had gone outside before I slipped up to the front. I wanted to do like he had told me and not make him angry again, but I felt like I had to know what was going on. You can understand that, can't you, Jake?"

"Sure," he said. He had skulked around in the dark himself for the same reason.

"Theodore left the front door open a little when he went out. I was able to hear them talking. I couldn't make out the words, but I heard the voices."

"Ted's—I mean Theodore's and the other man's?"

"And the woman, too."

Maxwell frowned. "Woman? What woman?"

"I don't know. I thought when I first looked out that there were two people in the buggy, not just one, and then after a few minutes, she said something. Her voice was very soft, even quieter than the others. But I'm sure it was a woman's voice. I couldn't see her. I couldn't see much of anything in the buggy, the canopy made it so dark."

His fingers tightening on the breech of the rifle, Maxwell asked, "You say you couldn't tell what they were talkin' about?"

"Not at all. I couldn't understand any of the words. But I heard three distinct voices. I know there was a third person."

"A woman . . ." Maxwell mused. "I wonder who the hell . . . Sorry."

"It's all right," Sandra told him. "Compared to some of the things Theodore's said to me, your language doesn't bother me at all, Jake. I like to hear you talk." Her own voice took on a strange huskiness as she spoke.

Maxwell wanted to get her mind back on what they had been discussing. "What happened then?"

"When I saw Theodore step away from the buggy, I figured the conversation was over and that I'd better get back to bed before he caught me spying on him. I hurried back through the store and into our bedroom. I almost knocked over a box of nails in the darkness, but I caught it in time. Only a few of them spilled, and I think I got them all picked up. Then I went back to bed and pretended to be asleep when Theodore came in."

"He believe that?"

"I've had a lot of practice at pretending to be asleep the last few months," she said, and Maxwell felt his face turning red and warm as he figured out what she was talking about. She continued, "I waited until Theodore was good and asleep again, then I slipped out and came over here to tell you what had happened. I didn't know you already knew about it."

"Didn't know about the woman," he said, his forehead creasing in thought. He couldn't think of anybody, man *or* woman, who would have a reason to come sneaking around and talking to Theodore in the middle of the night.

"What are we going to do?" Sandra asked.

"What can we do? Ain't against the law to talk to folks, even if it is mighty strange for 'em to come visitin' this late."

"But Theodore's doing something. Maybe something illegal."

She had just voiced the main worry that had been going through Maxwell's brain. It was a hell of a thing when a man was this suspicious of his own son, he thought.

"Reckon you could be right," he said slowly. "But even if he is, what do you *want* to do? He's your husband, after all."

"And I'm supposed to stand by him, no matter what he's done." Sandra sighed. "I've tried, Jake. I've tried to be a good wife to him. But it's hard when he treats me like . . . like he doesn't even love me anymore."

Maxwell wasn't sure Theodore had ever loved her. Maybe he had just married her so that folks could talk about what a pretty wife Theodore Maxwell had. The boy's mind seemed to work that way sometimes.

But he couldn't say that to Sandra, not as upset as she already was. And he didn't blame her for being upset. If Theodore wound up in trouble with the law, chances were she'd wind up part of it, too.

He didn't know what the devil to say, so he didn't say anything. He reached out in the darkness with his free hand and found her shoulder, soft and warm under the thin nightdress. He pulled her against him, let her rest her head against his chest. As they stood there, the heat of her body seeming to burn his skin, he awkwardly patted her back. Finally, he said, "I'm sorry."

She put her arms around his waist, hugged him tighter, lifted her head so that her lips grazed the line of his jaw.

From there it only took a second for their mouths to come together, and Maxwell was lost. There was no fighting it and damned if he even wanted to anymore. He let the butt of the rifle sag to the ground and then released the barrel, not even caring that it might discharge from being dropped that way. It didn't, but if it had, he might not have known it, wrapped up in Sandra the way he was.

This might make him the worst sinner on God's green earth, but he wasn't turning back this time. He couldn't. He didn't have the strength anymore.

There was a pile of hay in one of the stalls. Not the most comfortable bed in the world, he thought.

But it would do.

Chapter Nine

The hard riding, the running and jumping of the day before, had taken their toll on Nacho Graves. The wound on his side hadn't opened up again, but when he got out of bed the next morning he was extremely sore. Billy Cambridge saw the way he was moving as he came into the main room of the stagecoach station, and immediately a look of concern appeared on the lawyer's face.

"Looks like we won't be doing any more tracking today," Cambridge said from the table as he picked up his coffee.

"Because of me?" Nacho asked, a stricken look on his features. "But I'm fine, Billy. I feel healthy as a horse."

"A spavined old nag ready to be put out to pasture, maybe." Cambridge shook his head. "Sorry, Nacho. I won't risk your health like that."

"But, Billy, every day that goes by, the trail gets a little colder. It's going to rain, or the wind will blow hard, or both, and then those tracks will be gone forever. You don't realize how lucky we were, just being able to follow them yesterday."

"Yes, I do." Cambridge pointed at the bench on the other side of the table. "Now sit down and eat. Jake's got flapjacks and bacon on the stove. I'll bring you some."

Nacho sighed, shook his head in disgust, and sank onto the bench.

There was never any point in arguing with a lawyer, he thought. Billy had been pretty reasonable so far, but Nacho knew how easily he could get worked up and start flinging around two-bit words and acting like he was in a courtroom. Nacho could do without that.

He had to admit that he felt stronger after he ate. Jake Maxwell came in from outside just as Nacho was ruminating over the last of his coffee. The stationkeeper's face seemed more gaunt and hollow-eyed than usual this morning, and Nacho said, "You look like the night was not kind to you, Jake."

"Didn't sleep much," Maxwell said with a shake of his head. As if to change the subject, he asked quickly, "You boys goin' outlaw huntin' again today?"

"Nacho's in no shape for it," Cambridge declared, not giving his companion a chance to answer the question. "We'll have to postpone it again."

"That's a shame. I know you're anxious to find those owlhoots and get as much of that money back as you can. But if you're goin' to be around here today, maybe you can give me a hand with a little chore."

"Sure. We'd be glad for the chance to pay you back some for your hospitality. Wouldn't we, Nacho?"

The *vaquero* looked up. "What? Oh. Right. Anything we can do, just ask, Jake."

"I just need somebody to sort of keep an eye on the place," Maxwell said. "I'm runnin' a mite low on grain for the horses, and I need to get some. Nearest granary's about ten miles east of here at a little settlement called Antioch. There're no coaches due until late this afternoon, so there wouldn't be any chores you boys would have to do."

"Doesn't your boy Ted keep any grain over at the trading post?" Cambridge asked.

"Usually he does," Maxwell nodded. "But I checked yesterday. He's about out, too. I'll be picking up a load for him as well as for the station."

An idea occurred suddenly to Nacho, a way he might be able to escape a day of boredom sitting around the stage station. "Jake," he said, "why don't you let Billy and me go pick up that grain for you?"

Cambridge turned and glowered at him before Maxwell had a chance to respond to Nacho's suggestion. "Now what kind of an idea is that? I just got through saying that your health isn't good enough yet to go chasing outlaws again, and here you are volunteering to fetch a bunch of heavy sacks of grain."

Nacho leaned forward. He was no lawyer, but he had thought out his argument quickly and thoroughly. "At this granary, they have men to load the bags of feed, right, Jake?"

"Well, that's true," Maxwell admitted. "I usually pitch in and lend a hand, but you wouldn't have to."

"And you have a good wagon, don't you? A wagon with good springs that does not bounce its riders all around?"

Maxwell summoned up a grin. "It's a good wagon, sure enough. I ain't sayin' it's like ridin' on a cloud, but I reckon you'd be pretty comfortable."

Nacho turned back to Cambridge. "So you see, Billy, there is no reason we shouldn't go."

"You just want to see a town again," Cambridge said, narrowing his eyes in suspicion. "Maybe visit a saloon and flirt with a few pretty girls."

"It might help my injury," Nacho said solemnly. "A man in high spirits recovers faster, no?"

Cambridge replied dryly, "So I've heard." He took a deep breath. "All right, I don't suppose it would do any harm. But only if Jake agrees. What about it, Jake?"

Maxwell shrugged. "I don't care who goes and gets the grain, as long as I don't run out. I've got to keep the horses well fed and as healthy as possible."

Nacho's grin widened. "Then we go, right, Billy?"

"We go," Cambridge agreed.

Now that the question of who would pick up the grain was settled, it didn't take Maxwell long to hitch a team of mules to his wagon and drive it out of the barn. As he hauled the animals to a stop in front of the station, he asked Cambridge, "You sure you can handle these long-eared jackasses?"

"I've driven a mule team plenty of times before, if you remember right," Cambridge replied. He stepped up to the driver's seat and took the reins while Maxwell climbed down. Nacho followed the lawyer, settling down on the seat with a smile on his face. Even injured, he wasn't the type to sit around and do nothing. The prospect of having a job to accomplish again made him feel better right away.

"Don't know if Antioch was there the last time you came through this country or not, Billy," Maxwell said, "but it ain't hard to find. Just head south a little ways and take the cut-off that goes by the Baptist church. Stay on that road and it'll bring you right into the settlement. Granary's on the left as you go into town. Fella name of Barlow runs it. He knows my wagon, so just tell him you're pickin' up a load for me and one for the tradin' post. He'll fix you right up."

Cambridge nodded, then flapped the reins and shouted at the team. The mules hesitated for a second before stepping out in their plodding but steady gait. Nacho turned around on the seat, moving carefully so as not to put too much strain on the wound in his side, and lifted a hand in farewell to Jake Maxwell. Glancing past the stationkeeper, he saw Sandra step out onto the porch of the trading post. The morning sun struck highlights on her blond hair. She was unquestionably beautiful, Nacho thought.

But not as beautiful as Dove O'Shea.

As Nacho settled back on the seat next to Cambridge, he thought about the young half-breed girl. He wasn't sure why he felt such an instinctive attraction to her. Most men would be interested in that lithe body of hers, he supposed, but they would also be bothered by the scar on her face. Somehow, although he was well aware of it being there, it didn't make Dove any less appealing to him. She had experienced a great deal of tragedy in her young life, and now that he knew more about her, he decided that the expression in her dark eyes the day before had been one of haunting sadness. Maybe he was reading more into this than he should, he told himself. But that was all right; after all, he was impulsive, especially when it came to the *señoritas*.

"Well, you're about a million miles away," Cambridge said from beside him on the wagon seat, breaking into his thoughts and dispelling his mental image of Dove. "And from that little smile on your face, I'd wager there's a pretty girl there with you."

Nacho shrugged, the smile widening into a grin. He drew in a lungful of the crisp, cool air. "Just thinking that it's good to be alive on such a day," he said. "I nearly wasn't, you know."

"I seem to remember being there when you got shot," Cambridge said. "But you're going to heal up as good as new. I did quite a job of doctoring, if I do say so myself."

"Billy . . . Do you think we will really get that money back?"

Cambridge sighed. "I hope so. If we don't, I'm going to feel obliged to pay it back to Simon out of my own funds. It may take a while, but I can do it. Edward would probably offer to help me out, might even be willing to borrow against the ranch, but I'd never let him do that."

That was exactly what Edward Nash would do, Nacho thought. His *patron* and Cambridge had been friends and partners in the law practice for a long time. There was nothing Nash wouldn't do for Cambridge, and as his foreman, that same obligation held true for Nacho. But you could only help someone as much as they would let you.

Both men rode along in silence for a few minutes, but Cambridge spoke up again as the wagon reached the cut-off and he swung the team onto the other road. "I've been thinking about that O'Shea girl," he said.

"So was I, a little while ago."

Cambridge smiled. "Somehow, that doesn't surprise me. Anyway, I was wondering what she was doing over here at the Baptist church a couple of days ago. She never did explain that."

"Anybody can go to church." Nacho shrugged. "Even I have been to the mission in Pecos many times."

"Well, you've got a lot to confess. . . . The girl looked almost like a different person. Out there in the woods, she was almost all Comanche, but at the church she was as prim and proper as you please. I wonder which one is the real Dove O'Shea."

That was a good question, Nacho thought, and one he didn't have an answer for. He wouldn't have minded getting to know her better, though, and maybe he could figure it out, given enough time.

A little later, Nacho spotted the steeple of the church up ahead and pointed it out. "You said we wouldn't be here next Wednesday to have dinner with them," Nacho commented, "but at the rate we are going, we might be."

"I'm afraid you're right," Cambridge grunted. He inclined his head toward the whitewashed building. "Wonder who that is?"

A buckboard was coming up the short dirt road that led to the church, heading toward the main trail. A man and a woman were on the seat, and as Nacho and Cambridge came closer, both of them recognized the woman.

"That's Dove!" Nacho exclaimed.

"And the man with her is Reverend Livingston," Cambridge added. "That girl keeps turning up. This is three days in a row I've run into her."

He pulled back on the reins, calling to the mules to stop as they reached the spot where the church driveway joined the road. John Livingston brought his own team to a halt and smiled across at Cambridge and Nacho. "Good morning, gentlemen," he said heartily. "Mr. Cambridge, isn't it? You had dinner on the grounds with us a couple of days ago."

"That's right, Reverened," Cambridge replied. "How are you today?"

"Just fine, praise the Lord. Who's your friend, if you don't mind my asking?"

Dove answered the question. "His name is Nacho Graves," she said softly.

"That's right," Nacho said, taken a little by surprise. "Ignacio Alexander Rodriguez Graves, Reverend. Pleased to meet you." He tipped his hat to Dove and went on, "Good morning, Miss O'Shea."

Livingston said, "Pleased to meet you as well, Mr. Graves," then glanced curiously at the girl. "I wasn't aware that you were acquainted with these two gentlemen, Dove."

"They came to see my father yesterday," she said. "And of course, I saw Mr. Cambridge here at the church on Wednesday."

She was keeping her eyes slightly downcast, as any proper young lady would, and not looking directly at them. That was quite a contrast to the bold, none too friendly stare she had given them while holding a gun on them the day before. She wore a gingham dress, a lightweight shawl, and a sun bonnet, and the outfit and her attitude made Nacho understand what Cambridge had been talking about earlier. It was like this Dove and the buckskin-clad Comanche maiden were two completely different people. And yet they were unmistakably the same. There couldn't be two such women in the world, Nacho thought.

Surprisingly, he decided he preferred the Comanche version to the white. The dangerous, gun-toting girl in buckskin seemed more true to what he thought was Dove's actual nature. But he noticed that she didn't mention any details about their encounter the day before to the minister. Livingston probably didn't know what she was really like.

"Are you on your way to Antioch?" Livingston asked, and when Cambridge nodded, he went on, "So are we. The church is planning to build a baptistry instead of continuing to use the river or one of the creeks nearby, and Miss O'Shea is going to help me choose the fabric for the curtains. A new general store that should carry what we need recently opened in the settlement."

"Sounds like a fine idea, Reverend," Cambridge said. "We're on our way to pick up some grain for Jake Maxwell's stage station and his son's trading post."

Livingston's smile turned into a grin. "Why don't we drive along together, then? It'll give us all a chance to get to know each other better."

Nacho had been hoping for an excuse to spend more time with Dove O'Shea, but somehow he hadn't envisioned a preacher as part of the deal. Still, any chance was better than none. Quickly, he said, "Billy and I would like that, Reverend. Wouldn't we, Billy?"

"Sure," the lawyer agreed. "There's room for two wagons on this road. If we meet anybody coming the other way, though, we'll have to stop and let them pass."

Nacho wished Cambridge would stop worrying about such minor details. "Plenty of room," he said. "You'll see, Billy. Let's go, Jake's waiting for us to get back with that grain."

Cambridge gave him a sidelong look, then got the team of mules moving again. Livingston guided the buckboard alongside on the left. Wishing that he could somehow trade seats with Cambridge without looking too obvious, Nacho contented himself with leaning back slightly and looking past the attorney at the girl riding in the other vehicle.

Like most preachers, Livingston never seemed to be at a loss for words. As the wagon and the buckboard rolled along the trail, he told Cambridge and Nacho about his plans for the church. He had been called to serve as its pastor only a few months earlier, but already he was trying to put his own stamp on the congregation and the services. The weekly dinner on the grounds had been his idea, to attract more visitors—and therefore more potential converts. He also had in mind expanding the sanctuary itself, in addition to building a baptistry.

"Sand Ridge is a growing ministry, Mr. Cambridge," Livingston said proudly. "I expect to be spreading the Word of God for a long time around these parts."

"With your enthusiasm, I expect you're right, Reverend," Cambridge replied. He directed his next question to Dove—for which Nacho was very grateful. He hadn't counted on having to listen to Livingston all the way to Antioch. "Have you been attending services at Sand Ridge for very long, Miss O'Shea?"

"Not long," she answered with a shake of her head. Nacho watched the way the gesture made her long black hair sway as it hung down her back. "I was led to the Lord by Reverend Livingston."

"That's right," the minister said proudly. "Why, poor Dove was little more than a heathen savage when the hand of God guided her into our sanctuary one Sunday morning. She's half-Comanche, you know, and her father is this rough-hewn frontiersman. . . . Well, of course you know that, since you know Mr. O'Shea. I'm sure he's a fine man, but Dove and I have been unsuccessful so far in persuading him to attend services with us."

"I'm not well acquainted with Seamus O'Shea," Cambridge said, "but somehow I do have a hard time imagining him in church, Reverend."

"He'll see the light. Sooner or later, the Lord will work His wondrous way on old Seamus, just as He does with all of us poor sinners."

Nacho was rapidly forming a dislike for Reverend Livingston. The man was not only pompous and bombastic, he wouldn't let Dove join in the conversation. Maybe when they got to the settlement, Nacho thought, he would get the chance to have a word or two alone with her. He had a legitimate reason for wanting to talk to her—besides his usual habit of flirting with every pretty girl he ran across, that is. He and Cambridge were both convinced that Seamus O'Shea knew more about the outlaw gang operating in the territory than he had revealed the day before. If he could manage to get closer to Dove, that might lead to the information they needed to locate the owlhoots.

A little after mid-morning, the wagon and the buckboard reached Antioch. Traffic had been light on the road, and the two vehicles had managed to stay abreast most of the way. Now, as they entered the settlement, Livingston swung the buckboard to the right, crossing in front of the wagon as Cambridge held up his team momentarily. "See you in church, gentlemen?" he called.

"Maybe," Cambridge said.

Nacho waved at Dove as Livingston pointed the buckboard toward a newly-built general store. He noted the location of the mercantile and decided that once the granary workers were loading the feed onto the wagon, he would stroll over there and try to pry Dove away from the preacher for a few minutes. She didn't return his wave, but as he lowered his arm, she glanced back, and for the first time today, her eyes met Nacho's.

The dark-eyed gaze went right to the center of him. He couldn't read her expression, but he sensed the power of it. Then she was looking away again, and he felt the loss.

Yes, he was definitely going to have to get to know Dove O'Shea better.

"There's the granary," Cambridge said, pointing to a large building with a silo behind it on the left side of the road. "Like Jake said, it's not hard to find."

"Nothing in this town would be," Nacho commented. Antioch certainly wasn't very big, at least not yet. It had one main street and a couple of lanes branching off to either side. No more than a dozen businesses made up the heart of the town, and there were perhaps thirty houses scattered around. A man could stand in one spot, turn around in a circle, and see the whole community. Someday, if the town grew, it might turn into something more substantial. On the other hand, the people might all move away, and the abandoned buildings might fall into ruin. People thought of ghost towns as being connected with mining and rich veins that played out, but there were plenty of other reasons a settlement could die. A place like Antioch could go either way.

Cambridge brought the wagon to a stop in front of the granary. As he and Nacho were climbing down from the seat, a short, stocky man in a dirty jacket and a knitted cap came out of the building. "Somethin' I can do for you gents?" he asked. "Say, that's Jake Maxwell's wagon you're drivin', ain't it?"

"Jake said you'd probably recognize it," Cambridge replied. "He sent us to pick up a load of grain for the stage station and one for his son's trading post. You'd be Mister Barlow?"

"That's right."

Cambridge extended his hand. "Bill Cambridge. I'm an old friend of Jake's. We're staying at the station for a while, and we wanted to lend him a hand."

Barlow shook hands with him, then said, "I'll bet you're that lawyer fella. Heard about that stage hold-up and the money you lost. Mighty rough."

"Well, we haven't given up hopes of recovering it yet."

"Just as long as you don't hold your breath waitin' for Sheriff Massey to get around to it." Barlow got down to business. "I reckon this'll go on Jake's and Ted's accounts?"

"That's the way Jake wanted it."

Barlow nodded. "Me'n my brothers'll get busy loadin' you up, then."

As the granary operator turned to go back into the building, Nacho caught Cambridge's arm and said, "I think I will take a little walk, Billy."

"Over to the saloon? I only saw one in town. Or did you have a visit to the general store in mind?"

Nacho shrugged. "I might need to pick up a few things. A man can never tell."

"Go on," Cambridge said with a chuckle. "I'll keep an eye on things here." As Nacho turned away, the lawyer added, "You ought to be safe enough. I don't see how the O'Shea girl could hide a rifle in that dress of hers. A knife or a derringer, maybe."

"Billy!" Nacho sounded offended. "You misjudge her. She's really a sweet girl."

"She put the barrel of that gun against your spine and threatened to blow your head off," Cambridge reminded him.

"Well, I won't give her cause to do that again," Nacho declared firmly. "After all, we *were* sneaking around her father's house."

Cambridge nodded. "Just watch yourself."

Nacho straightened his jacket and ambled across the street toward the general store. As he went inside, he saw Dove and Reverend Livingston standing next to a counter on his left. They were looking through bolts of cloth that were spread out on the long surface. Dove had a look of concentration on her face as she tried to decide which fabric would be the most appropriate for the curtains in the church's new baptistry. Nacho thought the expression made her even more attractive—but he would have thought that no matter how she looked, he supposed.

"Hello again," he said, and both of them glanced up at him. He was only vaguely aware of the greeting that Livingston gave him, just as he was paying little attention to the other customers in the store or the white-aproned clerk who was standing near Dove and Livingston, waiting for them to make up their minds.

"I thought you came to town to buy grain, Mr. Graves," Livingston went on.

"Billy can handle that," Nacho said with a negligent wave of his hand. "I have more important things to do."

"Such as?" Dove asked, and he thought he detected a hint of mockery in her voice.

Solemnly, Nacho said, "I have come to buy licorice."

The clerk pointed a knobby finger toward another counter. "In that jar over there. Help yourself, mister, and I'll be with you in a few minutes to weigh it."

Nacho turned and tried to walk to the licorice jar with as much dignity as he could muster. It was the first thing he had thought of when Dove asked him what sort of important things had brought him into the store. He loved licorice, of course, and had ever since he was a boy, childish though it might be for a grown man to be eating the stuff. But it was hardly what anyone would consider a pressing errand.

He took the lid off the huge glass jar and had just reached inside when a voice said beside him, "I wouldn't mind having some licorice myself."

Nacho looked over and saw Dove standing there. Trying not to show his surprise, he said, "Of course. I'll get it for you."

He pulled a strand of the black, chewy stuff from the jar and handed it to the girl. She took it and said under her breath, "Thank you for not saying anything to the Reverend about yesterday."

"You mean about that gun you were waving around and using to threaten Billy and me?" Nacho asked quietly as he took out more of the licorice for himself. "I didn't figure it was any of his business."

He glanced past Dove and saw the clerk cutting a large piece off one of the bolts of fabric while Livingston looked on. The minister didn't seem to be paying any attention to the two of them.

Angry lights danced in Dove's dark eyes as she said, "Reverend Livingston may be my minister, but that doesn't mean he has to know everything about me and my father."

Eager to mollify her, Nacho said quickly, "Billy and I just thought that since you didn't bring up any of the details, we shouldn't, either. You see, *señorita*, we are not out to cause trouble for anybody except those lowdown hombres who robbed us."

"You still don't have any idea where to find them?"

"None," Nacho said with a shake of his head. "By now, they could be anywhere from Montana to the Rio Grande."

Dove nodded and keeping her voice low said, "I can see why you and Mr. Cambridge are upset about being held up. In fact, I was a little surprised to see you today. I thought you'd be out in the breaks again, hunting for those men."

Nacho put a hand on his side, over the bullet wound. "The injury would not let me ride today," he said dramatically. "Or at least Billy thought so. Now I can see that my pain was merely the instrument of a kind fate."

"A kind fate?" Dove frowned slightly. "I'm afraid I don't understand."

"If that bullethole hadn't been hurting like blazes this morning, Billy and I would not have come to this town on the errand for *Señor* Maxwell. And so we would not have run into you. As I said, fate is kind."

Dove blushed and lowered her eyes slightly, but a smile tugged at her mouth. The expression lit up her face, and once again it was as if the scar was not even there.

"I think you're a bit of a flirt, Mr. Graves."

"The best in all of West Texas. No, wait. I am the best *vaquero* in West Texas, that is it . . . I am the best flirt in all of the Lone Star State."

Dove gave a stifled giggle, sounding for all the world like a little girl. So that was one more facet of her personality, Nacho thought. She was a fascinating woman, and he was glad he had walked over here to the general store.

It would have been all right with him if the conversation continued indefinitely, but Dove said with a glance over her shoulder, "I have to get back to the reverend. I think he's almost ready to go."

Indeed, Livingston was carrying the thick roll of fabric toward the door. Dove smiled at Nacho again, then paused abruptly and looked down at the licorice in her hand, forgotten until now. Nacho waved her on and said, "I'll take care of it, *señorita*."

"Thank you," she called back. "Goodbye."

"*Hasta la vista*," Nacho replied, sadness welling up inside him at the thought of parting from her. Perhaps there would be another time. . . .

At that moment, Billy Cambridge came through the door, holding it open for Livingston and tipping his hat to Dove. "Finished your business, Reverend?" he asked.

"Yes, we have," Livingston replied. "What about yourself, Mr. Cambridge?"

"All loaded up and ready to go."

"Well, then, it seems as if Providence wishes us to be companions for a while longer, doesn't it? I trust you'll drive along with Miss O'Shea and myself back to the church?"

Cambridge hesitated, seeming to think about it, then grinned a little at the way Nacho was nodding so emphatically behind the backs of Dove and Livingston. "I think that would be a fine idea," the attorney said.

Quickly, Nacho paid the storekeeper for the licorice, then hurried out the door after Cambridge, Livingston, and Dove. Cambridge had pulled the wagon over in front of the store. It was loaded with big sacks of the grain that Maxwell needed for the stage line's horses.

As the four of them stepped up onto the vehicles, Livingston said, "I don't mind telling you, I'm grateful for the company, sir. Not only for the conversation, mind you, but because you never know when bandits will strike around here. But I think they'll be a great deal less likely to accost us while you and Mr. Graves are with us."

"Chances are they're still lying low after that stagecoach holdup," Cambridge said as he picked up the reins. "They might not pull another job for a couple of weeks."

Livingston shook his head. "You can never tell with miscreants like that, Mr. Cambridge. Evil men do things that don't always make sense."

"True enough, Reverend."

Nacho knew better than to expect many opportunities to talk to Dove on the return trip, not with the loquacious minister around, but he contented himself with looking at her and seeing the shy smiles she directed back at him. Her attitude was entirely different than it had been the day before, probably because the surroundings were so different, he thought. Out in the rugged country to the southwest, people had to be harder and colder to survive. Here, twenty miles to the east, there was less danger, less need to be hardbitten. That would account for Dove's new friendliness, the thawing of what Nacho had first taken to be a pretty icy personality.

Dove rode with the fabric on her lap, and Livingston talked more about the new baptistry. The cloth was heavy and thick and a subdued blue in color, entirely appropriate for its intended use, Nacho thought, although he didn't know much about such things. His mother had been Catholic, his father Episcopalian, but you couldn't go very far in Texas without tripping over a Baptist or two. And anytime you ran into more than two Baptists, one of them was bound to be dunking the others in a river or a creek. Nacho sometimes wondered if they took turns. Theology, he supposed, was one of those mysteries he'd never figure out—like women.

He was looking at Dove and musing about such things when the shooting started.

Chapter Ten

Nacho's head jerked around as the gunshots blasted through the morning air. The wagon and the buckboard had rounded a curve in the trail a couple of minutes earlier, and now a dozen men on horseback were boiling around that same bend, dusters flapping and the rifles in their hands barking viciously.

"It's the same gang!" Nacho shouted as he reached for the Colt on his hip.

Cambridge slapped the reins hard against the backs of the mules and yelled, "Hyyaahh!" at them. To Livingston, he called, "Get that buckboard moving, Reverend!"

Grimacing as he twisted around on the seat, Nacho threw a glance toward the other vehicle. Dove's face was pale as she looked back at the pursuers. Even a girl as self-reliant and competent as she no doubt was would be more than a little nervous to see a gang of hardcases like that coming after her. Anger surged up inside Nacho.

The outlaws would pay for what they had done to him, but more importantly, he would have vengeance on them for frightening Dove O'Shea!

Slugs whined overhead, the sound mixing in a sinister harmony with the explosions of gunpowder. The mules finally broke into a jolting run, and next to the wagon, the buckboard was also traveling faster now. In the fleeting glance he spared Livingston, Nacho saw that the preacher's lips were moving. Probably uttering a prayer, the *vaquero* thought.

Praying was fine. But shooting straight came in handy, too.

Nacho squeezed off a shot.

It was going to be hard to hit anything; as a difficult platform for shooting, a swaying, bouncing wagon seat ran a close second to the saddle of a galloping horse. But he was going to discourage the men chasing them as much as possible. He was the only one who could put up a fight. Cambridge and Livingston were busy with their respective teams, and Dove was unarmed. He found himself wishing she had that Spencer carbine she'd poked into his neck the day before.

The outlaws had closed the gap considerably during the moments it had taken for Cambridge and Livingston to get their teams running. Now the riders were less than a hundred yards back and coming still closer. Nacho fired again, knowing all too well that his targets were out of range. He had plenty of shells in his belt loops, though, and he wanted the outlaws to know he was armed.

He could see the bandannas tied over their faces as masks, the tips of the colorful scarves fluttering in the wind. The men were still too far away to recognize as individuals, but Nacho was sure this was the same bunch that had stopped the stagecoach. He squeezed off his third shot.

Over the thunder of galloping hooves, Cambridge shouted, "Nacho! That grove of trees up ahead!"

Nacho looked around. The terrain on both sides of the trail was fairly open along this stretch, but fifty yards ahead, a clump of live oaks sat to the right of the road. Nacho knew right away what Cambridge was planning, and he gave the lawyer a nod. There was no way the heavily loaded wagon could outrun the men on horseback, and it was unlikely the buckboard could, either. The only other alternative was to fort up and try to fight off the outlaws, and those trees were the closest cover.

"The trees, Reverend!" Cambridge yelled at Livingston, but Nacho wasn't sure whether or not the minister heard. Livingston was sawing back and forth with the reins, and his eyes were wide with panic as he glanced back at the pursuing gang. Obviously, he wasn't accustomed to anything much more dangerous than his congregation dozing off during the sermon. Cambridge waved toward the live oaks, trying to get his attention.

Nacho's mouth was a tight line. None of the shots being fired by the gang were coming close enough to worry about right now, but sooner or later they would catch up and their marksmanship would improve. If he and Cambridge took cover in the trees and Livingston didn't, the outlaws might decide to continue after the easier prey.

Why the devil were the owlhoots after them in the first place? he wondered. Trying to waylay travelers like this was the mark of a gang desperate for money. The outlaws should have had plenty of loot left over from their last job. After all, it had been less than a week since they had stolen twenty thousand dollars.

Like the preacher had said, though, there was no telling what evil, greedy men would do. Nacho started to fire again, then eased off the pressure on the trigger. He only had two bullets left in the cylinder of the Colt, since he always kept one chamber empty, and he wanted to save them until the last minute before the wagon reached the trees. Once he and Cambridge had some cover between them and the outlaws, he would have a chance to replace the spent cartridges.

And in a case like this, he was going to load six, by God!

The wagon jolted roughly as Cambridge veered right and swung it off the trail. Nacho hung on tightly with his left hand as he emptied the Colt in his right, trying to brace himself against the seat back so that his body wouldn't be jerked from side to side. So far, the wound in his side didn't seem to be bleeding again.

Of course, if the bandits caught up with them, he would have a lot more to worry about than a single bullet graze.

Thankfully, Livingston seemed to have gotten the idea. The buckboard followed the wagon, circling behind the trees. Cambridge yanked his team of mules to a stop and dropped from the seat. Nacho followed. Livingston was hauling back frantically on the reins, trying to bring the horses to a halt before they went too far and dragged the buckboard out of the shelter of the trees. Seeing what was happening, Nacho leaped forward and grabbed at the two horses' harness. He set his feet, digging the high heels of his boots into the dirt. The added weight made the team stop just short of the open.

Cambridge took Dove's arm and helped her down from the seat of the buckboard, then hustled her around to the other side. Crouched there, she had not only the trees but the bulk of the vehicle between her and the outlaws. Cambridge crouched at the rear corner of the buckboard, his gun up and ready.

Nacho darted around the horses, hoping they weren't so skittish that they'd take off again. The stolid mules weren't just about to stampede once they had stopped. Livingston was still on the seat of the buckboard, so Nacho reached up to grab the sleeve of his coat.

"Get down off there, Reverend!" he said urgently, pulling on the pallid-faced minister.

With a little shake of his head, Livingston seemed to realize what was going on. He practically rolled off the seat, stumbling as his feet hit the dusty ground. He might have fallen if Nacho hadn't had hold of him.

"Stay down!" Nacho told him. The *vaquero* could still hear the hoof-beats of the horses bringing the outlaws closer and closer, and when he peered over the buckboard, he caught glimpses of them through the trees.

"We've got to slow them down, Nacho," Cambridge said. "Come on!"

The lawyer left the shelter of the buckboard and ran into the trees. His gun began barking. Nacho hesitated just long enough to look down at Dove and say, "If they get past us, you and the reverend take cover between the buckboard and the wagon. It's not much, but it's the best we can do."

She jerked her head in a nod. Nacho could tell how frightened she was, and he wanted to take her into his arms and comfort her, tell her that every-thing was going to be all right. But there was no time for that and anyway, it would be a lie. He didn't know that everything was going to be all right, not by a long shot.

He darted into the trees to join Cambridge. Pressing himself behind the trunk of one of the live oaks, he thumbed open the Colt's loading gate and began ejecting the spent shells, then reached for fresh cartridges.

The trunk wasn't wide enough to conceal all of his body, and he felt terribly exposed. None of the trees were big enough to serve as really effective cover. Nacho forced the fear to the back of his mind and glanced around the trunk. The outlaws were about thirty yards off, and they were pulling their horses to a halt.

"Hit any of them, Billy?" Nacho called to Cambridge.

The lawyer shook his head. "Range is too damned far. Watch out, Nacho! They're going to sit back there and cut loose with those rifles!"

Nacho crouched, then stretched out on the ground behind the tree as the Winchesters began their spiteful cracking. Slugs tore through the branches over his head with a wicked sound, and he wasn't just about to look up to see how close they were coming. He hoped Dove and Living-ston had the sense to stay down.

"This is hopeless!" Cambridge said during a momentary lull in the firing. "They can keep us pinned down as long as their ammunition holds out. We're outgunned, all the way around."

"That didn't stop you and the other Rangers in the old days," Nacho reminded. "*Los Tejanos Diablos* never gave up."

Cambridge looked over and gave him a grim smile. "You're right. I may not be a Texas Ranger anymore, but I don't feel much like surrendering." With that, he rolled slightly to one side, lifted his revolver, and began firing at the outlaws as fast as he could work the hammer and trigger.

Nacho joined in, and to his surprise he saw their slugs begin to kick up dust near the feet of the outlaws' horses. The animals shied nervously, and the riders lowered the rifles and tightened their reins, pulling the horses back a little. Then, as Nacho and Cambridge watched in amazement, the outlaws wheeled their horses and spurred them into a gallop, riding away from the grove of trees and their intended victims as fast as they could.

"What the devil . . .?!" Cambridge exclaimed.

"They're pulling out!" Nacho said.

"Don't be too sure of that," Cambridge warned. "Could be this is some kind of trick."

It quickly became obvious that it wasn't, however. The outlaws disappeared back down the trail, vanishing almost as quickly and unexpectedly as they had shown up.

"What's happening?" Livingston called in an anxious voice. "Why has the shooting stopped?"

Cambridge and Nacho both stood up. "The outlaws are gone, Reverend," Cambridge replied to the questions. "Looks like they gave up."

Livingston peered over the buckboard with a look of disbelief on his face. "Gone?" he echoed. "Then we're safe?"

"That seems to be the case."

"Praise the Lord! Our prayers were answered."

As Nacho watched the rapidly dissipating cloud of dust that had been raised by the gang's departure, he wondered if Livingston might be right. They had been outnumbered, outgunned, and pinned down in bad cover. It must have been divine intervention that had made the outlaws turn tail and run.

Somehow, though, he had a hard time believing that. There had to be something else, some other reason. . . .

"The important thing is that we're all safe," Cambridge said. "You and Miss O'Shea aren't hurt, are you?"

"I'm fine," Dove replied. "A little shaky, perhaps, but I'm not wounded."

"None of the bullets touched me, either," Livingston said. "The hand of the Lord turned them aside."

"That, or poor aim," Cambridge muttered so that only Nacho could hear him. Nacho could tell from the look on the lawyer's face that Cambridge was very puzzled by what had just happened.

"Maybe they were just playing with us," Nacho suggested. "You know, trying to throw a scare into us."

"Well, if that was the case, they succeeded admirably." Cambridge reloaded his gun and then holstered it. "We'd better get moving again before they change their minds and come back."

Nacho agreed completely with that suggestion. He seized the opportunity to help Dove up onto the buckboard, taking her arm as he did so. This was the first time he had actually touched her, and he was amazed at the way the warmth of her flesh came right through her clothes. If he hadn't already been a little winded from all the excitement, she would have taken his breath away.

Without wasting any time, they got the two vehicles moving again, and the rest of the trip back to the church was uneventful. There was no sign of the outlaws along the way.

"I think we'll be safe enough now," Livingston said as he brought the buckboard to a stop in front of the sanctuary. "I hate to think about what might have happened if you and Mr. Graves hadn't been with us, Mr. Cambridge. Those thieves would have surely been disappointed with any booty they could steal from us, and they might have taken their anger out on Miss O'Shea."

"I'm just glad we were in the right place at the right time, Reverend. You might consider taking some of your male parishioners with you next time you have to travel around the countryside. Unless that gang has been apprehended by then, of course."

"That's a fine suggestion, brother. Good day to you . . . and thanks again."

Cambridge touched the brim of his hat, then got the mules moving again. Nacho waved, and this time, Dove returned the gesture. There was a silly grin on his face, Nacho knew, but he couldn't help it.

After a couple of minutes, Cambridge said, "Looks like you made a little progress. That girl was downright friendly to you today. That's a far cry from threatening to kill you."

"Ah, Billy, you just do not understand women. One day they want to kill you, the next day they are in love with you." Nacho shrugged. "It is all part of their feminine charm."

"Hold on a minute. I said she was friendly. I didn't say she was in love with you."

"But isn't it obvious?"

Cambridge snorted. "About as obvious as the reason behind that attack on us."

Nacho glanced over at him. "What do you mean, Billy?"

"I mean there's something mighty strange going on around here. There was no reason for that gang to jump us." The lawyer inclined his head toward the load of grain in the back. "You think they were after that?"

"Well . . . no."

"And Livingston and the girl didn't have anything worth stealing with them. Actually, your idea about them chasing us just for the fun of it makes as much sense as anything. But I don't think they'd do that, either."

Nacho had to agree. If these were the same men who had held up the stage—and he was still convinced that they were—those desperados weren't the type to be pulling such pranks. They had been deadly serious about their work.

"If they were really trying to kill us," Nacho mused, "they would not have left like that. We might have downed a few of them when they closed in, but they would have gotten us. The same thing is true if they were after Dove and the preacher for whatever reason."

"That's right. So we're left with something that doesn't make any sense at all—but it almost got us killed anyway."

Nacho sighed. His side hurt a little, and so did his head. He was a simple man, he told himself, and unaccustomed to all this heavy thinking.

"Billy . . ." he said, "I am starting to wish we had taken the train."

Theodore Maxwell stood on the porch of the trading post and looked out at the night. There was more of a chill in the air this evening than there had been previously, and Theodore was glad he was wearing a jacket.

He glanced over at his father's stage station. A southbound coach had come through earlier, meaning that the place was a beehive of activity for a little while, but the stagecoach was long gone now and the station was quiet again. The glow of a lamp came through the windows of the building. Supper would be over, and more than likely, his father and the two visitors would be sitting around discussing the morning's run-in with the outlaws.

Theodore had heard all about it from Sandra after lunch. He had pretended disinterest, but actually he had listened keenly to everything she had to say. According to her, Cambridge and Graves had narrowly escaped death at the hands of the desperados, and Reverend Livingston and that half-breed O'Shea girl had been in danger, too.

It was a shame the two men from West Texas hadn't caught bullets, Theodore thought. That would have simplified matters a great deal. He was getting tired of their poking around.

He was getting tired of other people's suspicions, too, come to think of it.

The door of the trading post opened and someone stepped out onto the porch behind him. It had to be Sandra; there weren't any customers in the place at the moment. After a few seconds of silence, she asked, "What are you doing, Theodore?"

"Getting some air," he said. "Anything wrong with that?"

Hastily, she answered, "No, not at all. I was just wondering—"

"Nothing to wonder about," he interrupted sharply. "A man wants a little air, he steps out and gets some. All there is to it."

"Of course."

Still without turning to face her, he went on, "Why don't you close the store for the night? I don't think we're going to get any more customers."

"We usually stay open a little later than this," she began tentatively.

"I don't care, dammit! I said we're closed for the night. Go ahead and lock up and then go to bed."

"Will . . . will you be coming along soon?"

He pretended he hadn't heard the question as he went down the two steps to the ground. There was a small barn behind the trading post where he kept his horse. He intended to throw a saddle on the animal now and take a ride, but he wasn't going to explain that to Sandra. She had no right to know everything about his comings and goings, he thought.

She didn't call after him or ask any more foolish questions. That was the way he liked it. She would learn to keep her nose out of his business—or she would regret it for the rest of her days.

When he rode away from the trading post a few minutes later, he headed north, following the road toward the Red River. Fallen leaves crackled under the horse's hooves as Theodore kept it at a steady trot. At this time of night, the trail was practically deserted. It was unusual whenever he met anyone during one of these nocturnal rides.

He had been to enough of these nighttime rendezvous that he had no trouble recognizing the proper place to turn off the road, even in the darkness. Making his way along an even narrower trail, in a few minutes he reached a bluff overlooking the broad, shallow river. He could see starlight reflecting off its muddy, slow-moving surface.

As he drew rein, a voice said, "Right on time, Maxwell."

Theodore started, involuntarily jumping a little in the saddle and then mentally cursing himself. He didn't want the other man to think that he was nervous. He shouldn't have reacted that way, he told himself. After all, he had been expecting the man to meet him.

"I try to be punctual, Graham. Now do me the favor of telling me why you insisted on this meeting."

A man on horseback moved out of the shadows of the trees into the faint light of the moon and stars. Theodore could make out the flat-crowned hat and the long duster, the right hand flap of which was pushed back at the moment to allow the man easy access to his gun. Theodore swallowed. When Asa Graham wore his duster like that, trouble was usually in the offing.

"Take it easy," Graham advised. He was doing something with his hands, and a moment later Theodore found out what. The outlaw tipped a cigarette into his mouth and reached into his shirt pocket for a light.

"You're not going to strike a match, are you?"

"Why the hell not?" Graham asked around the cigarette. He found a lucifer and scratched it into life. It threw harsh illumination over the hard planes of his face as it flared up and he held the flame to the cigarette. "There's nobody around to see me but you."

Trying to suppress his impatience as Graham casually shook out the match, Theodore said, "Look, I've done everything you've asked of me. If you want something else, all you have to do is tell me. I'll do it if I possibly can."

"Yeah, you've done a good job, Maxwell," Graham drawled. "You've helped us get rid of some of the money and goods we've stolen. But don't start thinkin' that gives you the right to order folks around. Somebody else is callin' the shots in this operation, and don't you forget it."

Theordore's impatience was turning into irritation now. "I'm well aware of that," he snapped, "and I'm not trying to give orders."

Graham drew in on the cigarette, making the tip glow. As he blew the smoke out, he said, "Reckon you heard about that lawyer and his Meskin pardner gettin' shot at today. We were tryin' to throw a scare into 'em. You know whether or not it worked?"

"If you mean are they going to give up their quest to recover the money you stole from them—no, they aren't. In fact, from what I hear I'd say they're more determined than ever to catch up to you."

"Damn!" Graham rasped. "I don't know why the hell I didn't just go ahead and kill those bastards when I had the chance. That'll teach me, won't it?"

"What happened today? Instead of trying to scare them off, why didn't you just kill them then?"

Graham shook his head. "We had orders to shoot high and back off after we'd shook 'em up a mite."

"Was that all you wanted from me?" Theodore asked. "Just to find out if Cambridge and Graves were planning to give up?"

Graham shrugged and said, "That's it."

"And for that you dragged me off up here to the river?"

The outlaw's voice hardened as he replied, "It wasn't my idea. I do what I'm told, just like you—most of the time, anyway."

"Well, tell the boss that I'm getting tired of this arrangement. I can play a bigger role in all of this, and I want a face to face meeting with him to talk about it."

Graham gave a short bark of laughter. "You sure you want me to pass along that message?" he asked. "You're forgettin', Maxwell—havin' you workin' with us may come in handy sometimes, but we could get along without you just fine."

Theodore took a deep breath and controlled his temper with an effort. "Just tell him."

"Whatever you say." Graham turned his horse around and rode back into the shadows, disappearing within a few seconds.

Theodore stayed where he was for several moments, his hands clenched tightly on the saddlehorn. He hated being forced to deal with a crude, uneducated killer like Graham, but for the moment that was all he could do if he wanted to remain a part of the gang's lucrative activities. He sighed again and lifted the reins, ready to turn around and ride back to the trading post.

The rattle of dried leaves made him stop short.

His muscles tensing, Theodore sat up straighter in the saddle and peered around him in the night, listening and looking intently. He had a small pistol shoved into the top of his boot—he seldom went anywhere without it these days—but the little revolver didn't have much stopping power. Suddenly he wished he had brought along a bigger handgun or a rifle.

Again the rustle of leaves came to his ears, and this time he was able to pinpoint it better. The telltale sound came from his right, from a thick clump of brush. With his pulse hammering wildly in his head, he reached down, pulled up his pants leg, and plucked the pistol from his boot. "Who's out there?" he demanded as he straightened and leveled the gun at the bushes. "Who's spying on me, dammit?"

There was no answer, and Theodore suddenly found his anger overwhelming his fear. He spurred forward, sending his mount crashing through the brush. Moonlight flashed on something light-colored to the right. Theodore jerked the muzzle of the gun in that direction and his finger started to tighten on the trigger.

"No! Don't shoot!"

He stopped at the last instant as the familiar female voice pleaded with him. "Sandra?" he gasped in surprise, dropping out of the saddle and grabbing at her. His fingers caught the shoulder of her dress and jerked her closer to him.

Her terrified face stared up at him, the blue eyes wide with fear.

Theodore began to smile as he felt coldness seeping through his body. "Come along, my dear," he said in deceptively gentle tones. "We're going to have to talk about this."

Chapter Eleven

Sandra had never known horror like she experienced during the ride back to the trading post. Theodore said little as he forced her to show him where she had hidden her mount. The horse was an old mare they had used for plowing when Sandra had put in a garden back in the spring. It was a little surprising the mare had even been able to keep up with Theodore's saddler, but Sandra had been determined to find out once and for all where he was going when he disappeared like this. She had followed him at a distance, finally dismounting, tying the mare, and slipping the last hundred yards on foot.

What she had heard was bad enough—her husband involved with the gang of vicious outlaws that had been plaguing the area for weeks—but even worse was the fact that she hadn't been able to sneak away without alerting him. She had considered waiting until he was gone to emerge from her hiding place in the bushes, then decided against the idea for fear that the mare would whinny at Theodore's horse when he passed. The presence of another horse so close to the rendezvous would have alerted him, too, so she had taken a calculated risk and tried to get away first.

But that risk had backfired on her, and now she was the prisoner of a man she didn't even know anymore. Certainly, Theodore wasn't the same man she had married.

Or maybe he was, and she suddenly realized that might be the worst thing of all.

"Mount up," he had told her. "We're going home." When she had pulled herself up onto the old saddle he had taken in trade from a farmer who didn't have the price of some supplies, he had reached over and grabbed hold of the reins.

Now, as he led the old mare along the road back toward home, Sandra shuddered as she thought about what might happen once they reached the trading post. Surely he wouldn't kill her. If he had wanted to do that, he'd had his chance when he first found her. She had been able to tell from the way his features contorted in the moonlight as he recognized her that he wanted to kill her. She had closed her eyes tightly and waited for the bullet that would end her existance.

The bullet hadn't come, and now she had to worry about what might take its place.

Maybe it would help to talk to him, she decided desperately. Summoning up her courage, she said, "You don't have to worry about me, Theodore. I . . . I won't say anything. You're my husband. I'd never say anything to hurt you."

Without glancing over at her, he asked, "You won't say anything about what?"

"Why, about you and that outlaw, of course! About you working with that gang!"

She thought a smile played fleetingly across his lips; it was hard to be certain because they were passing through some shadows cast by trees beside the road. But when they emerged from the gloom, his features were frozen again in their usual dour expression.

"So you were close enough to hear what we were saying," he commented, almost as much to himself as to her. "I thought so, but now I'm sure."

"No," she said quickly. "I didn't hear anything—"

"It's too late, Sandra. You gave in to your impulses one too many times. You followed me, trying to satisfy your curiosity. That was a mistake."

"I swear to you—"

"That won't help," he cut in coldly. "You have to learn your lesson."

She bit back a sob. He sounded more cruel and callous than ever before. She would never survive this night. She was sure of that now.

But she would hang on to life as long as she could.

He wouldn't be expecting any resistance from her; he figured she was too cowed for that. No sooner had that thought raced through her head than she was acting on it. She leaned forward, snatching at the reins he was using to lead her horse, and at the same instant, she dug the heels of her shoes into the mare's flanks. The animal leaped ahead, shocked by the unexpected prodding.

The loosely-held reins slipped through Theodore's fingers. Sandra felt him try to tighten his grip on them, but he was too late. She had them again, and she used them to jerk the horse toward the field alongside the road.

"Run! Oh, God, run!" she shouted to the mare, leaning forward and slashing at her with the trailing ends of the reins. She hated to treat the old horse this way, but her only hope of escaping from Theodore lay in opening up a quick gap that he couldn't overcome. He still had his gun, but she knew he wasn't a good enough shot to hit her, not at night and not from the back of a running horse.

The mare responded gallantly, stretching her legs out and surging to more speed than Sandra thought she had in her. Behind her, Sandra heard a faint, surprised curse. She twisted her head around long enough to see Theodore starting after her in pursuit, then she concentrated on guiding the horse through the rough field.

Not surprisingly, Theodore didn't shoot at her. He was aware of his limitations with a gun, she knew, and besides, he wouldn't want a bunch of shots to alert the countryside that something was going on. She understood now that whatever form his vengeance took, he wanted it to remain quiet and unnoticed.

She glanced back again, unable to keep herself from checking to see how close he was. He had shaved a little off her lead, but he wasn't overtaking her as fast as she had been afraid he would. That was due to the mare's courageous effort, Sandra thought. But how long could the horse keep running like this?

Not long, she discovered to her dismay a moment later as one of the mare's front legs suddenly buckled. Sandra jerked in the saddle as the horse stumbled and threatened to go down. She made a grab for the saddlehorn but missed, and before she could make another try, the saddle itself went out from under her as the mare fell.

Instinctively, Sandra kicked her feet free of the stirrups. When she was little, she had seen a man dragged by a runaway horse, had seen another man with his leg pinned and crushed underneath a fallen mount. She let go of the reins and let herself pinwheel through the air, trying frantically to find the ground so that she could land properly.

The ground found her first. Her shoulder slammed into the earth, and it was only blind luck that sent her rolling in a way that lessened the damage done by the fall. When she came to a stop, she was numb from the impact and breathless as well, gasping for the oxygen that had been forced out of her lungs when she crashed into the ground.

Over the pounding of blood in her head, she dimly heard a bone-chilling sound—the screaming of a horse in pain. Forcing the muscles in her neck to work, she lifted her head and made out the dark bulk of her horse nearby. The mare was thrashing around and trying to get back on its feet, but the broken leg wouldn't let it. While she was racing across the field, Sandra realized, the horse had stepped in some sort of hole.

Hoofbeats made her look past the injured mare, and she saw Theodore galloping toward her. The fear that had filled her earlier came flooding back, galvanizing her muscles. She was on her feet almost before she knew what was going on, then turning and running. . . .

Her flight was hopeless, and within a matter of seconds, it was over. Theodore rode up beside her, his horse almost driving its shoulder into her. Sandra cried out as she stumbled and fell again, landing heavily in grass that was beginning to turn brown with the approach of winter. Theodore reined in and swung down from the saddle, and seconds later, his fingers dug painfully into the flesh of her arms as he hauled her to her feet.

His palm cracked across her face, stunning her. He was trembling with rage as he shouted, "Filthy slut! I'll teach you to spy on me, you God-damned bitch!" Again and again he slapped her, until the fiery, stinging pain of the blows went away and Sandra's face was as numb as the rest of her. Then he shoved her away and stood there watching, his chest heaving with exertion and emotion, as she fell again.

She tasted dirt in her mouth, and she pushed it out with her tongue as she sobbed, "Don't . . . don't hit me . . . don't hit me anymore . . . ."

He didn't seem to hear her. "Teach you a lesson," he muttered, standing over her. "Ought to just go ahead and kill you. But I won't. You'll keep your mouth shut, won't you, Sandra? You'll be a good wife and not say anything about this to anyone, won't you?"

"Won't say . . . anything," she made herself respond. "Jus' don't hit me. . . ."

She heard him laugh, and then he stalked away. A moment later, a gun cracked and the squealing that was coming from the mare stopped.

Maybe that was what he should do for her, she thought fuzzily. Maybe a bullet through the brain would be better.

But instead, he came back, grasped her arm, and jerked her roughly to her feet. Something twinged inside her, a pain she hadn't noticed before. A broken rib? That was possible. It didn't really matter, not anymore.

"Come on," Theodore grated. "Now that you've gotten that out of your system, we're going home. It'll be slower now. We'll have to ride double."

She cringed at the thought of having to be that close to him all the way back to the trading post. But her mind was beginning to work a little more clearly now, and she pushed away the thoughts of how welcome death might be. She was still alive, and she was determined to stay that way. It was better to share a horse with Theodore than to be left out here dead.

Because as long as she was alive, she still had hope, no matter how faint it might be.

Hope that somehow she would have her revenge on the man she had married.

Dawn wasn't far off when Asa Graham reached the cabin, deep in the rugged, wooded breaks, that the gang used for a hide-out. Graham was tired from the long ride he had made tonight, and when one of the other outlaws who was on lookout duty challenged him, he answered peevishly, "It's me, you damn' fool. Ain't you got eyes in your head?"

"Sorry, Asa," the man said. "I thought it was you, but I figured it was better to be sure than to let some lawman ride up on us, especially since the boss is here."

"The boss is here?" Graham repeated in surprise. "What for?"

"To find out what you learned from Maxwell, I reckon."

Graham nodded. "Yeah, that makes sense. Guess I better get this over with."

He rode into the small clearing around the cabin. Dismounting in the grayish light, he turned his horse into the pole corral and then stepped up onto the porch.

A figure sat in an old rocking chair at the far end of the porch, shrouded in shadows. In a cold voice, the head of the gang asked, "Did you talk to Maxwell?"

Graham strolled along the porch, trying to look more casual than he felt. He was a cold-blooded killer, but even he felt a little touch of unease at this moment. He said, "I talked to him."

"And?" The question came at him sharply.

"Cambridge and Graves ain't givin' up. At least that's the way Maxwell heard it. I reckon those West Texas boys ain't very smart."

"Too damn smart, that's more like it. If they keep snooping around, they'll figure things out. They might even find this hide-out."

Graham began, "I don't think that's very likely—"

"I don't give a damn what you think! I don't want to take the chance."

"So go ahead and kill them," Graham shrugged, stung by the rebuke.

"I may have to." After a moment, the figure in the rocking chair went on, "Did Maxwell have anything else to say?"

Graham chuckled, his mood improving. "Yeah, he did. He said he wanted a bigger piece of the pie. Wants to meet with you face to face so the two of you can talk about giving him more to do. And more money; I reckon that's what he's really after."

There was silence on the porch for several seconds, then: "The Goddamned fool. He already knows more that it's safe for him to know."

"That's the way I see it, too," Graham nodded. "Maxwell's gettin' ambitious, and that ain't good."

"You think he could be a threat to us if he doesn't get his way?"

"Damn straight." Graham's tongue came out of his mouth and wet his lips. "You want me to kill him?"

Again there was silence as the question was pondered. Finally, the answer came. "Not yet. His services have been valuable. But if one more incident occurs to make us think Theodore Maxwell has outlived his usefulness . . . then, yes, you can kill him. But be sure and make it look like there's no connection between him and us. Let it be during an attack on the trading post, something that people will put down as just another outlaw raid."

"Sure. That won't be hard to manage, if it comes down to that. And I reckon it will."

"We'll see. I suppose that's all for now." The figure stood up. "I'll be in touch."

Graham nodded and remained on the porch long enough to watch the boss ride away into the dawn. Folks would be mighty surprised, he thought with a chuckle, if they knew who was really ramrodding this gang.

Then he went inside to get some sleep. He needed his rest; killing was tiresome work.

Jake Maxwell was up early, as usual. Cambridge and Nacho were still in their bunks asleep by the time Maxwell had tended to the stock and gotten breakfast started. He was in the habit of rising early anyway, and considering how badly he was sleeping these days, the less time he spent in his bed, the better.

He stepped to the front door of the stage station and peered over at the trading post in the morning light. The place looked quiet, almost deserted. Maxwell frowned slightly. Theodore usually had the store open by now, so that he wouldn't miss any customers who happened to come by this early. Maxwell hoped that nothing was wrong over there, that Theodore hadn't found out what had happened between him and Sandra.

Maxwell sighed. Two nights had passed since he and Sandra had given in to the demons that plagued them. Demons of lust, that was what a preacher would call them. Maxwell knew he and Sandra had sinned. But it was hard for him to understand what was so wrong with two lonely people taking some comfort in each other. The laws of God and the laws of Man both said that what they had done was evil.

But Maxwell just couldn't quite see it that way.

Still, until he could sort things out in his mind and figure out what to do next, he was glad that Sandra seemed to be avoiding him. She hadn't come over to the stage station the day before, and Maxwell was grateful for that. He wouldn't have known what to say to her. She would probably be mighty embarrassed, too.

The creak of door hinges caught his attention. He looked up and saw Sandra stepping out on the porch of the trading post. Maxwell noticed the stiff way she was moving, like something was hurting her. She had a broom in her hands, and she started sweeping off the dust that had accumulated on the porch overnight.

Theodore emerged from the building behind her, put his hands on his hips, and looked around at the morning in what seemed to be great satisfaction. For some reason, the boy's expression made Maxwell bristle. Folks who looked that proud of themselves usually didn't have much to be proud of, he thought. Theodore glanced toward the stage station, but if he noticed his father standing at the door, he didn't give any sign of it. He turned his head and said something to Sandra.

Maxwell's eyes narrowed. Unless he was mistaken, Sandra had flinched when Theodore spoke to her. The boy had to be bad-talkin' her again.

What he ought to do, Maxwell told himself, was to march over there, grab Theodore by the collar and the seat of his pants, and fling him in the water trough. Then he'd tell the fool youngster to treat his wife right for a change. Somebody needed to teach Theodore a lesson, and by God, Jake Maxwell was just the man to do it! It was his duty as a father.

But even as Maxwell stiffened in anger, he knew he wasn't going to do any such thing. The time when something like that might have done some good was long past. Theodore was going his own way now, and nothing his father could say or do would make a difference anymore.

Theodore turned and went back into the store, leaving the door open behind him. Sandra kept sweeping, her head drooping and her eyes on the floor of the porch. Maxwell wanted to call out to her, but he didn't. He took a deep breath and started to swing around to enter the stage station.

That was when Sandra looked up.

Maxwell felt like someone had slugged him in the belly. Even at this distance, he could see the ugly bruises on Sandra's face. Those bruises, and the pained way she was moving around, told him that she had been on the receiving end of a brutal beating. There was only one person who could have given her such a thrashing.

Theodore . . .

Maxwell was stalking across the clearing between the stage station and the trading post before he knew what he was doing. His weathered features were set in a furious, outraged mask. His callused, knobby fingers clenched into fists. Theodore had finally gone too far.

Sandra shook her head urgently, and finally the look of pleading on her face penetrated the fury that had thrown a red haze across his vision. As he reached the bottom of the steps, she said softly, "Go back, Jake! Please go back."

"But you're hurt," he began. Now, up close, it was almost more than he could stand to look at the marks on her. A shudder ran through him. How dare Theodore do such a thing?

"I'm all right," she whispered. "Please . . . I don't want him to see me talking to you."

"He's got to be punished," Maxwell said, talking about his son as if Theodore was still a child. "Somebody's got to teach him a lesson. . . ."

Sandra caught her breath sharply at those words. Maxwell didn't understand why, but obviously they bothered her. Before he could go on, she said, "I'll meet you later, in the barn. Please, Jake. I've got to talk to you, but I . . . I can't do it now."

He felt himself nodding. The last thing he wanted to do was to cause more trouble for Sandra. "In the barn," he agreed.

"As soon as I can." She darted a glance over her shoulder, afraid Theodore would appear out of nowhere.

Maxwell nodded again and turned around, heading back to the station building. As he walked away, he thought he heard his daughter-in-law stifle a sob, and it was difficult not to rush back to her, fold her into his arms and promise her that nothing would ever hurt her again. But somehow he kept walking.

Billy and Nacho were still asleep, he saw as he passed through the station building. He moved quietly so as not to disturb them, both for their own sake and for his. He didn't want any witnesses to his meeting with Sandra. He already felt guilty enough without his friends knowing what was going on.

Maxwell went straight through the station and out the rear door, heading for the barn. His heart was still thudding heavily in his chest, not only from his anger at Theodore but also because he was about to be alone again with Sandra. Even under the circumstances, he couldn't help but be excited by her.

As he waited in the barn for her, the minutes seemed to stretch out unnaturally. He hoped that Theodore hadn't found out she was coming here to meet him. Maxwell had no idea what had happened to set him off and cause the violence he had inflicted on Sandra, but it was obvious now that Theodore couldn't be trusted. It was hard to believe that the baby boy Maxwell remembered so clearly had grown into such an evil man, but there was no denying the facts.

Maxwell was pacing back and forth impatiently when he heard the door of the barn open slightly. He stopped short and turned around as Sandra slipped through the narrow opening. She closed the door behind her, plunging the inside of the barn into shadows again. Some light filtered down from the windows in the loft, but it didn't do much to relieve the gloom. Even in the dim illumination, Maxwell could see the bruises. Without thinking about what he was doing, he held out his arms to Sandra, and she came into his embrace without hesitation.

Burying his face in her hair, Maxwell tightened his arms around her, easing off quickly when a sharply indrawn breath reminded him that she was hurt. He started to say, "I'm sorry—"

"It's all right," she cut in. "Go ahead and hold me. Just hold me, Jake."

That's what he did for the next few minutes, lifting a hand to pat her lightly on the back or stroke her hair. She rested her head against his chest and sighed. Maxwell tried to listen closely for any sounds coming from outside, so that Theodore or the two visitors wouldn't be able to walk in and surprise them, but he found himself swept away in the sensations of warmth and softness that he held in his arms.

"Why?" he finally murmured, as much to himself as to Sandra. "Why would anyone . . ." He couldn't complete the question.

But she could. She asked, "Why would anyone do such a thing?" Then she spat out the answer. "Because he's an outlaw, just like those men who stole your friend's money."

Maxwell leaned back and placed his hands on her shoulders. He asked, "What are you sayin', Sandra?"

"It's simple enough. Theodore is part of that outlaw gang that's been making life miserable for folks around here."

Blinking in astonishment, Maxwell studied her face. Her eyes and the set of her mouth told him she was telling the truth. "How do you know this?" he demanded.

"I saw him and heard him. He met another member of the gang up by the Red River last night. I followed Theodore and heard all of it. He's been helping them get rid of the things they steal."

Once Sandra got started, the story tumbled out of her in a hurry, from her trailing Theodore to the rendezvous, to her capture by him later and the beating he had given her. Maxwell's anger grew. It had been hard at first to accept the idea that his son was a criminal, but there was no doubt in his mind that Sandra was telling him what had really happened. Theodore might not be stopping stages and robbing people at gunpoint, but he was just as much an owlhoot as the other members of the gang.

"I swore to him that I'd never tell anyone," Sandra said as she finished her story. "But I couldn't keep the truth from you, Jake. You had to know."

"Damn right," he growled. "Something's got to be done about this. Theodore can't go on helpin' those desperados loot the territory. And he's got to pay for what he did to you, too."

"He said he was teaching me a lesson." Sandra had to choke out the words.

"He's the one goin' to learn it," Maxwell promised grimly. "I'll horse-whip him—"

"If you do, he'll try to kill you. We've got to wait, Jake, and figure out the best thing to do."

"We could go to the sheriff and tell him about what Theodore's been doin' with those bandits."

She shook her head. "It would be my word against his. Yours wouldn't carry any weight in court, since you didn't actually see or hear anything yourself. All he'd have to do would be to deny the whole thing and claim that I was making up stories about him because he beat me. Who do you think the sheriff would believe in a case like that?"

"Reckon he'd likely believe Theodore," Maxwell grunted, a bleak look on his face. He sighed. "Reckon you're right, Sandy. We're goin' to have to do some studyin' on this. But I know just the man to help us—Billy Cambridge."

"If . . . if you tell Mr. Cambridge, he might figure out . . . what's been going on between us."

"Doesn't matter," Maxwell said with a shake of his head. "I'm willin' to face that if you are. Theordore's turned into a hydrophobic skunk, and he's got to be stopped."

After a second's hesitation, Sandra nodded. "You're right. He's got to be stopped. We'll tell Mr. Cambridge about it—about all of it."

Carefully, so as not to hurt the rib that might be cracked, Maxwell hugged her again. He had heard some newfound strength in her voice when she spoke those last words.

He hoped she could hang on to that strength during the rough times that were coming.

Chapter Twelve

Billy Cambridge woke up suddenly, his hand going to the gun under his pillow. But the hand on his shoulder that had shaken him awake belonged to Jake Maxwell, he saw, and Maxwell was saying hurriedly, "Hold on, Billy, it's just me."

Cambridge grunted, sat up, and rubbed his eyes. "Old habits," he said. Then, seeing the anxious expression on Maxwell's face, he went on, "What's wrong, Jake?"

"Plenty. Soon as you're dressed, Sandy and I need to talk to you."

"Sandra?" Cambridge frowned. No more information came from Maxwell, though, so he shrugged, got out of the bunk, and reached for his pants. "What about Nacho? Do you want him in on this meeting, too?"

Maxwell nodded. "Reckon he's got a right, seein' as how those owlhoots shot him."

The lawyer's frown deepened. What could this have to do with the outlaw gang? Could Maxwell have discovered something about them?

By the time Cambridge was dressed and emerging from his cubicle, Nacho was coming out of his own room, knuckling sleep from his eyes. He looked at Maxwell and said, "What is this all about, Jake?"

Sandra Maxwell was seated at the long table, her back to Cambridge and Nacho. Maxwell motioned for them to come around the table, and as they did so, both men stopped in their tracks. Sandra looked up at them, the dark bruises on her face standing out in hideous contrast against her fair skin.

Nacho let out a surprised curse in Spanish, and Cambridge said, "Oh, my God. What happened?"

"That boy of mine is what happened," Maxwell said. "He did this to Sandy, probably cracked one of her ribs, too."

Nacho's chivalrous nature was aroused to fury by what he saw. Sputtering in his anger, he said, "We should tie him to a horse and drag him!"

"What good would that do?" Cambridge asked sharply.

"Well . . . he wouldn't be in any shape to mistreat a woman for a long time!"

"It wouldn't change anything, though." Cambridge tried to be objective, to force his own feelings of outrage into the back of his mind. Sitting down on the bench a few feet from Sandra, he asked, "Has this sort of thing been going on for very long?"

"Theodore never did *this* before," she answered in a quiet voice. "We haven't . . . gotten along well for quite a while, but I was never really afraid for my life with him—until last night." Her mouth twisted bitterly. "I suppose in his mind, he had a good reason for what he did."

"What reason could ever be good enough to do such a thing?" Nacho demanded.

She looked up and met their gazes. "I found out Theodore is an outlaw."

"What?" Cambridge exclaimed.

"He's working with the same gang that held up the stagecoach and robbed the two of you."

As Cambridge and Nacho sat and listened with astonished looks on their faces, she gave them the same story she had told Maxwell. Cambridge's mind was turning over rapidly as Sandra filled in the details. Although it was hard to believe that his old friend's son had turned out so badly, the story made sense. He glanced up at Maxwell's stony features, a pang of sympathy shooting through him.

When Sandra was finished, Maxwell said, "I thought you and Nacho ought to know about this, Billy. For one thing, we're not sure what we ought to do about it."

Nacho spoke up. "I'm sorry that your son is mixed up in this, Jake, but we have to go to the law—"

"No," Cambridge said.

Nacho looked at him in puzzlement. "But Billy, I thought you were the one who said we had to do everything according to law."

"That's exactly my point. We don't have enough solid evidence against Theodore, and we don't have anything to lead us to the rest of the gang."

"But Sandra saw him with one of the outlaws, probably the one who shot me!"

"That's true, but her testimony alone wouldn't be enough to convict Theodore." Cambridge glanced at Sandra and Maxwell and saw them nodding. "You've already thought of that. Good. Then you understand why it wouldn't do any good to go to the sheriff with this."

"We were hopin' you might come up with an idea, Billy," Maxwell said.

Cambridge leaned back and nodded toward the stove. "I could use a cup of that coffee that's brewing over there. Might wake me up a little more and help me think."

Maxwell fetched coffee for all of them, but when he put a cup in front of Sandra, she shook her head and stood up. "I can't stay," she said worriedly. "I've already been away from the trading post for too long. Theodore might be getting suspicious." She hesitated. "Jake, would you check out the back door and see if he's anywhere in sight?"

"Sure." Maxwell went to the rear door and stepped out for a moment, then returned to say, "Don't see the boy anywhere."

"I'll slip over to our barn, then go into the store from there. He'll think I was just attending to my chores . . . I hope."

Maxwell stepped aside to let her through the back door, and as she passed him, he reached up and let his hand brush her shoulder for a second. There was something about the gesture . . . an intimacy, a warmth . . . that struck Cambridge as strange. Nacho didn't seem to notice.

Maxwell came back to the table and picked up his own coffee. "Biscuits'll be done in a bit," he said. "Now, Billy, what do you think we should do?"

"What do you want to do?" Cambridge asked in turn. "If you warn Theodore that you're on to him, he might give up his involvement with the outlaws."

"You mean let him get away scot-free?" Maxwell shook his head. "I can't do that, even if he is my son. Not after what he did to that poor girl."

Cambridge nodded grimly. "I was hoping you'd say that, Jake. Because I'd like to use Theodore to help corral the rest of the gang."

"You mean to set some sort of trap?" Nacho asked. "Trick him into leading us to them?"

"Not exactly. I don't think Theodore knows where their hide-out is, any more than we do. The fact that he met with one of the gang at such an out-of-the-way place indicates that. I figure they'd want to keep him in the dark about such things as where they're hiding and who's actually leading the gang."

"You don't reckon that Graham fella is the boss outlaw?" Maxwell asked.

"Not if Sandra was reporting the conversation between Theodore and Graham accurately. Someone else is the ringleader, and I have a pretty good idea who."

The other two men leaned forward, waiting to see what Cambridge was going to say.

"Seamus O'Shea," the attorney declared.

Maxwell stared at him for a moment and then shook his head. "We've talked about this before, Billy. Seamus's done some bad things in the past, but he ain't got that in him these days. I reckon he's truly sorry for what he did when he was ridin' with the Comancheros."

"I know you're fond of him, but everything points in his direction. He knows this area, and he's bound to still have some outlaw contacts from the old days. He'd be able to put together a gang and run it."

"Maybe so, but I still don't believe it."

With a solemn expression on his face, Cambridge asked, "Would you have believed that Theodore was part of the gang if Sandra hadn't caught him red-handed?"

A muscle in Maxwell's cheek twisted as a grim look settled over his face. He took a deep breath and slowly shook his head. "Reckon not. I knew something was wrong, but I'd never have guessed that he was mixed up with outlaws. Maybe you're right about Seamus, Billy."

Now Nacho leaned forward, obviously disturbed. "What about Dove?" he asked.

"O'Shea's girl? What about her?"

"Do you think she knows what her father is doing, Billy?"

Cambridge shrugged. "No way of knowing for sure. Probably not, I'd say. She seems like a pretty level-headed young woman, but sometimes a child has a blind spot when it comes to her father. Anyone as devoted to the church as Dove is, though, I can't see her keeping it to herself if she found out who was behind all the robberies around here."

"Well, at least you aren't accusing her of being part of the gang."

With a smile, Cambridge said, "I don't think that's very likely."

Maxwell got up to take the biscuits out of the oven, but as he did so, he asked, "What do we do now?"

"I'll go over to the general store in a little while and pick up some more supplies," Cambridge said. "While I'm talking to Theodore, I'll let it slip that we've got a good lead to the outlaws and expect to locate their hide-out in the next few days. Theodore and the gang are bound to have some way of communicating, so I'm betting that he gets a message somehow to them. From what Sandra said, I'm hoping that their system is so primitive that a face to face meeting will be required for Theodore to pass on the warning to them."

Nacho spoke up, understanding now what Cambridge had in mind. "So we keep an eye on Theodore, and when he has his rendezvous with somebody from the gang, we follow that hombre back to the hide-out."

"Exactly," Cambridge nodded.

"Could work," Maxwell admitted. "I hate settin' a trap, though. The worst part is always the waitin'."

"That's true." Cambridge smiled and pointed toward the stove. "That's why I think we should help pass the time with some of those biscuits of yours."

Nacho brightened up immediately, the prospect of more trouble forgotten in his hunger. "And some of those apricot preserves!" he suggested.

As Cambridge had said, the waiting was difficult. Nacho stalked impatiently around the stage station all morning, hoping that the lawyer would soon decide the time was right to throw out the bait to Theodore Maxwell. Finally, a little before noon, Cambridge picked up his hat and put it on. "Let's take a little stroll over the trading post, Nacho," he said.

"Good luck," Maxwell said tightly as Nacho reached for his own hat.

It was hard to imagine what the man was going through, Nacho thought as he and Cambridge stepped outside. Even though it was obvious that Maxwell and Theodore weren't close, and probably hadn't been for a long time, they were still father and son. It had to hurt to help set a trap for your own son. Justice demanded that the outlaws and their accomplice be brought in, but Nacho wasn't sure Maxwell would have been able to do what he had done—if Theodore hadn't crossed the line by beating Sandra so brutally.

As Nacho and Cambridge strolled across the open space toward the trading post, the *vaquero* saw a familiar buckboard parked in front of the store. It was the vehicle belonging to the Sand Ridge Baptist Church, he realized after a few seconds. His pulse jumped. Maybe Dove was inside the trading post, picking up a few things for the church. She seemed to be Reverend Livingston's unofficial assistant, so that was possible.

To Nacho's disappointment, Dove hadn't come along on this trip, he saw as he and Cambridge entered the store a moment later. Livingston was standing at the counter in the rear, talking to Theodore Maxwell. Sandra was nowhere in sight, and Nacho figured she was staying in the living quarters in the back of the building most of the time. She wouldn't want people to see her, not with those ugly bruises on her face.

Livingston turned as the footsteps of the West Texans announced their presence. The minister smiled and nodded. "Good morning, gentlemen," he said affably. Theodore just looked at them, not venturing a greeting of any kind.

"Well, pastor, you look like you've gotten over that little dust-up the other day," Cambridge said.

"No point in worrying about that now. The hand of the Lord protected us. I have faith He will continue to do so."

Nacho nodded toward the bag sitting on the counter in front of Livingston. "I thought you bought your supplies in Antioch."

"Only the things that Brother Maxwell here doesn't have available," Livingston replied. "The trading post is much closer."

"Where's Miss O'Shea today?" Cambridge asked the question that Nacho had been working up to.

Livingston shook his head. "I don't know. I'm sure I'll see her at services tomorrow, but she has her own life to lead. She only helps me out when I have a chore that requires a woman's touch."

That made sense, Nacho thought.

The preacher went on, "Well, I've got to be going, now that I've stocked up on provisions. Good day, gentlemen." He swung the bag off the counter and turned toward the door.

Nacho stepped forward quickly, an idea occurring to him. He said, "Let me help you with that, Reverend."

"But I can handle it just fine—"

"I insist. Back home as a boy, I used to help out the padre at the mission all the time."

Livingston shrugged and handed over the bag of supplies. "All right. Thank you, Nacho."

Cambridge gave his friend a puzzled glance, then turned his attention back to Theodore. "We could use a few things, too," he began, and Nacho knew he would work the conversation around to the outlaws, then subtly throw out the bait and set the trap for Theodore. It would be easier for Cambridge to do so, Nacho had realized, if the talkative Reverend Livingston was out of the way. Even though Livingston had picked up his supplies to depart, Nacho knew his type. He might stretch out his leave-taking for several minutes.

Hefting the bag, Nacho headed for the door, and Livingston had no choice but to follow, leaving Cambridge alone with Theodore.

When he reached the buckboard, Nacho placed the supplies in the back of the vehicle, then turned to Livingston. The minister smiled and said, "Again, my thanks, Nacho." He paused, then continued, "Can I count on seeing you in church tomorrow?"

Nacho hesitated before shaking his head. "I do not think so, Reverend," he answered. "Billy and me, I think we are going to be busy. We have a good lead on the men who robbed us."

A look of intense interest appeared on Livingston's face. He leaned forward, picking up on Nacho's quiet, confidential tones as he asked, "You've found the gang that attacked us on the trail?"

"Well . . . not yet." Nacho glanced at the trading post. "But we found out that someone around here is working with them."

"Impossible!" Livingston exclaimed, still keeping his voice low. "I know most of the people around here. They're law-abiding, God-fearing folks."

"Most of them, maybe, but not all, Reverend." Nacho hesitated again, wondering just how much to tell Livingston. After all, the preacher had a stake in this, too. The gang had chased him and shot at him, for whatever reason, most likely just because he'd had the bad luck to be traveling with the two visitors from West Texas. And as a man of the cloth, he would also want to see the criminals brought to justice, Nacho reasoned. He went on, "Billy is setting a trap for the bandits right now."

Livingston looked baffled. "But Mr. Cambridge is in the store talking to Theodore—" He broke off and shook his head, eyes widening. He whispered, "Theodore Maxwell? Allied with a band of desperados? I don't believe it!"

"You can believe it," Nacho said grimly. "It's true. We're counting on him to help lead us to the others."

Livingston shook his head, obviously having trouble taking in all this surprising news. "What about his father?" he finally asked. "Does Jake know?"

Nacho nodded. "I'm afraid so."

"I have to go talk to him, pray with him. He'll need a friend with him in this time of trouble."

Reaching out to catch Livingston's coat sleeve, Nacho stopped the minister. "I don't think that would be a good idea right now. Better to wait until it's all over."

"Well . . . maybe you're right. Do you know who's leading the gang?"

Nacho thought about what Cambridge had said about Seamus O'Shea, but he also considered the fact that Livingston associated closely with O'Shea's daughter. If the reverend let anything slip to Dove before the trap was ready to be sprung, she might warn her father. He agreed with Cambridge that Dove likely didn't know anything about what O'Shea had been doing, and her emotions would be terribly torn if she discovered he was still an outlaw. Would she help him escape justice, or would she stand by and watch him be killed or captured and sent to prison? Either way, it would be a horrible experience for her. Nacho wanted to postpone that as long as possible.

"No," he said in reply to Livingston's question. "We don't have any idea who's in charge."

"You probably will soon enough." Livingston put a hand on Nacho's shoulder. "Thank you for telling me this, brother. I feel like everyone around here is part of my flock, whether they attend the church or not, and a minister has to be ready to help out whenever trouble comes. I'm going to go back to the church and pray about this right now, so that the Lord can show me the right path to follow."

"Sure, Reverend. But keep it between you and God, all right? We don't want those hombres getting wind of the fact we're on to them."

"Of course," Livingston promised. He stepped up to the seat of the buckboard and reached for the reins. "Good luck, Nacho. As they say out in your part of the country, *Vaya con Dios.*"

Nacho grinned and gave a little wave as Livingston drove off. The

minister was a little stuffy and a little too full of religious fervor sometimes, at least as far as Nacho was concerned, but despite that he was
all right.

Cambridge emerged from the trading post as Nacho turned back
toward the door. The lawyer was carrying a bag of supplies, too,
although not as large as the bundle of goods Livingston had pur-
chased. Cambridge had borrowed the money for the supplies earlier in
the morning from Jake Maxwell, so that he would seem to have a
legitimate reason for visiting the store and talking to Theodore.

The two men walked side by side toward the stagecoach station. As
soon as they were out of earshot of the store, Nacho asked, "How did
it go?"

"Fine," Cambridge replied. "Theodore got real interested when I
dropped the hint that we had a lead on the location of the outlaws'
hide-out. He tried to pry that out of me and was even pretty open
about it. But I put him off, told him we didn't want to say much about
it until we knew for sure—which I said would be within the next few
days, so he'll know it's urgent that he contact that fella Graham."

"You think this is going to work, Billy?"

"I don't see any reason why it shouldn't, assuming that Sandra was
telling us the truth.

"She was," Nacho asserted. "I know women, Billy, and Sandra was
telling us the truth, no doubt about it."

"Well, considering your unfailing instincts for reading the fairer sex,
that makes me feel better," Cambridge said dryly. "I suppose you
knew it way ahead of time when that señorita in Fort Stockton was
going to come after you with a meat cleaver."

Nacho scowled. "That was different," he insisted. "She was loco.
I'm always right about women—as long as they are not crazy."

"I see. And that schoolteacher in Pecos . . . She was loco, too?"

"Well, no," Nacho said uneasily. He seized on the answer he was
looking for. "But she was from Boston! That's almost the same thing."

"And that actress who came through town with that traveling show
troupe?"

"But she never told me she was married! Her husband, he was the
one who was loco! Chasing me around with that wooden sword and
yelling about the bows and arrows of outrageous fortune. . . ." Nacho
shook his head. "Actors don't count, either, Billy. You got to be fair."

Cambridge nodded. "All right. You're the best judge of women's characters that I've ever seen, Nacho. Fair enough?"

Nacho accepted the assessment solemnly. "Fair enough."

Chapter Thirteen

Nacho, Cambridge, and Jake Maxwell took turns keeping an eye on the trading post during the afternoon. Maxwell insisted on doing his part, and Cambridge didn't argue with him. Now that Maxwell had seen Theodore's villainy for himself, the lawyer reasoned, better to let him take an active part in settling the messy situation. That would be less painful in the long run.

A great many customers came and went at the trading post. Maxwell was able to identify quite a few of them, but that left plenty of strangers, including some hard-faced men who drifted in alone and left the same way.

"That's not unusual," Maxwell said when Cambridge mentioned it, confirming what Cambridge himself had already noticed during his and Nacho's stay at the stage station. "This is the main road runnin' north and south in these parts, and there's several trails headin' east around here, too. Not to mention the smaller ones goin' west, through the breaks, although folks don't use them as much. Drifters ride through all the time."

Nacho was at the stove, checking on the stew that was simmering for supper. He looked up and asked curiously, "Why are you so interested in a bunch of saddle bums, Billy? We see more than our share of them in Pecos, too."

"Yes, but I figure that's how Theodore gets his messages to the gang," Cambridge replied. "One of the outlaws rides up, buys something, and then passes a high-sign to Theodore if there's a meeting. It works the same way in reverse. If Theodore has something to say to Graham, he gives a signal to the messenger and then meets Graham later up by the river."

Maxwell looked doubtful. "You're sayin' that one of them outlaws stops at the tradin' post every day?"

"No, I don't think that's likely," Cambridge said shaking his head. "They probably have some sort of schedule, though, so that one of the gang—a different one each time, so that people will be less likely to recognize him—comes by every few days. They wouldn't need to be in constant touch with Theodore, but they probably do check in a couple of times a week. He met with Graham last night, which means the gang's messenger was here yesterday to let him know about the rendezvous. That's why I said it would probably be a day or two before our plan will do any good. We've got to keep an eye on Theodore now, though, just in case I'm wrong about some of the particulars."

"I'm glad you're along to do all this heavy thinking, Billy," Nacho said with a grin. "Me, it makes my head hurt."

Maxwell paced back to the window where he could see the trading post. "Well, I'll be glad when it's all over," he said bleakly. Both Nacho and Cambridge looked at his sagging shoulders with sympathy, then exchanged a glance. Nacho shrugged, and shook his head. Life took some mighty strange twists sometimes.

If Theodore passed along a message during the afternoon, the watchers had no way of knowing it. But he stuck close to the trading post, never venturing any farther than the barn. Sandra came outside once, cast a quick look toward the stage station, then looked away just as quickly. Nacho happened to be on lookout duty at the moment, and he felt that he could sense the girl's despair and desperation even at this distance. He wished there had been some way to get her out of there and keep her out without alerting Theodore that something was wrong. Everything had to stay as normal as possible, until they had a chance to trail Graham back to the hide-out.

They took turns through supper, one man watching while the other two ate. Then Nacho helped Maxwell change the team on a northbound coach that came through during the evening, while Cambridge stayed at the window. Theodore seemed to be going about his business normally, as if he didn't have a care in the world. Full darkness settled down, and the hour wound on toward nine o'clock.

"The boy'll be closin' up soon," Maxwell commented, his voice showing the strain of this long day. "He sometimes stays open until ten, but not usually. One of us might ought to slip out where we can keep a better eye on his barn. He might be able to sneak out of the tradin' post without us seein' him, now that it's dark, but he couldn't ride off without us hearin' him."

Cambridge nodded. "That's a good idea. You want the job, Nacho, or would you rather I did it?"

Nacho was at the window again, pulled back to one side of it so that he could edge an eye past the facing and see the trading post without being too obvious. He said, "I'll go, Billy. I've had more practice being quiet."

"Not likely," Cambridge snorted. "I was fighting Indians before you were born, my friend, and when you fight Indians, you've got to adopt their tactics if you're going to win. I remember a time when the Ranger company I was in had to slip up on a Comanche village . . ."

"Wait a minute, Billy," Nacho said sharply as he peered through the window. "I always like to hear your stories, but I think you better come look at this. Riders coming."

"Coming where?" Cambridge asked as he got up from the table. "Here? Or the trading post?"

Nacho shook his head. "I don't know, but I don't like the looks of this." A curse ripped out of him in Spanish as he grabbed for the gun on his hip. "It's the *bandidos!*"

Cambridge and Maxwell bolted to his side and peered out the window with him. A dozen men on horseback had ridden into the area of light cast by the lanterns burning on the front porch of the trading post. They wore the distinctive dusters and had bandannas tied over their faces. Nacho even recognized some of the horses.

"What the hell!" Cambridge muttered. "Are they planning to hold up the place?"

There were a couple of horses and a wagon tied up in front of the trading post, all of them belonging to customers. If gunplay broke out now, those customers might come rushing out of the store and into the path of the bullets. Nacho's grip tightened on the butt of his Colt. He wanted to open fire on the riders, but he held down that urge for the time being, until they saw what was going to happen.

"Why'd they ride up there bold as brass?" Maxwell asked.

"I don't know, but we'd better blow out that lamp, or they'll notice us looking out at them," Cambridge said. Nacho ran over to the table and blew out the lantern. Now, with no light behind them, they could watch the outlaws without being noticed.

Nacho picked out the leader of the gang, the tall man with pale hair hanging down the back of his neck. That was the man who had shot him. The *vaquero's* temper surged up again, and Cambridge must have sensed his tension.

"Easy, Nacho," the lawyer breathed. "We'll know what they're up to soon enough."

Indeed, the riders were swinging down from their saddles and handing their reins to one of the members of the gang. The others drew their guns and went up the steps to the porch, then strode into the trading post.

"They're raidin' the place," Maxwell breathed. "Sandy's in there . . . !"

He whirled around and dashed across the room, snatching the Winchester that hung on pegs beside the front door. "Jake!" Cambridge cried, but he was too late. The stationkeeper threw the door open and plunged out into the night.

Nacho ran after him, saying over his shoulder, "It's too late for plans now, Billy. We got to stop them!"

As he ducked through the door, Nacho heard Cambridge behind him. Maxwell was already halfway across the open space between the stage station and the trading post. So far, the outlaw who had been left with the horses hadn't noticed his approach, but that changed in the next few seconds. The man heard the pounding of running footsteps and spun around. The light from the porch shone on the blued steel barrel of the gun in his hand.

Maxwell didn't slow down or try to swerve, just ran straight on, a target that was getting better by the second. He wasn't thinking about anything except reaching Sandra. Nacho knew that he was liable to run right into a bullet unless something happened to distract the outlaw.

Jerking to a stop, Nacho lifted his Colt and triggered it, sending a bullet past Jake Maxwell. The outlaw's pistol boomed a second later, but the bullet screamed off into the night. Nacho's shot hadn't hit anything, but it had distracted the man enough to make him miss.

The twin explosions jolted some sense back into Maxwell. He went to one knee, lifted the Winchester, socketed the butt against his shoulder, and squeezed off a shot. The crack of the rifle was followed by a yell of pain as the outlaw was thrown backward by the bullet crashing into his shoulder. He let go of both his gun and the reins, and the horses started milling around, made skittish by the gunfire.

"Spread out!" Cambridge called. Nacho veered to the right while the lawyer went to the left. Maxwell was on his feet again, charging toward the front door of the trading post, the leading point of the attacking triangle.

Shots broke out inside the store, a fusillade that was mixed with screams and shouted curses. Nacho offered up a prayer as he raced toward the right end of the porch. It sounded like Graham and the rest of the gang were slaughtering everyone in there.

Suddenly, several of the duster-clad owlhoots came boiling out the door. They spotted Maxwell and triggered off several shots at him, forcing the stationkeeper to throw himself to the side. Maxwell rolled behind the shelter of the parked wagon.

Nacho snapped off a shot as he reached the end of the porch. He caught a glimpse of Cambridge as the lawyer made the left end. They would have the outlaws in a crossfire now as they emerged from the door of the trading post. Nacho fired again and saw one of the outlaws stagger, a bright red stain blooming on the shoulder of his duster. Muzzle flashes winked from the other end of the porch as Cambridge opened fire.

Tucking back around the corner of the building as the bandits flung lead back at him, Nacho crouched, counted three, and then emerged to squeeze off two more shots. That emptied his Colt. He ducked behind cover again and reached for the loops on his shell belt to reload.

As he thumbed fresh cartridges into the cylinder, he heard the crack of Maxwell's Winchester again. From the sound of it, the stationkeeper was giving a good account of himself. As Nacho let the loading gate snap shut, Maxwell shouted, "Sandy!"

Darting out from behind the building, Nacho saw flames through the big window in the front of the store. Bright yellow-red tongues of fire were shooting up all through the place, and smoke began to billow out through the open door. The porch was on fire in a couple of places where stray bullets had shattered the hanging lanterns. The smoke from the fire and the haze of powdersmoke in the air made it hard to see as the outlaws leaped from the porch and tried to catch their horses. Nacho started to shoot again, then eased off on the trigger when he realized he couldn't see what he was shooting at. If the bandits had taken hostages—and he certainly wouldn't put it past them—then his bullets might hit an innocent prisoner. He couldn't take that chance.

Cambridge's six-shooter had fallen silent, too, and so had Maxwell's Winchester. Somewhere in the smoke-choked darkness, Maxwell shouted Sandra's name again. Nacho heard hoofbeats and knew some of the gang were getting away. A moment later, boots pounded on the planks of the porch and Maxwell cried once more, "Sandy!"

Nacho jammed his Colt back in the holster and placed a hand on the porch. He vaulted up, ignoring the pain from the wound in his side. He'd hurt it so many times since the hold up that the twinges of pain were getting to be like old friends to him. Trying to wave some of the smoke away from his stinging eyes and leaping around the small fires, he made his way toward the front door.

The inside of the store was like a scene from a fire-and-brimstone preacher's version of hell. Flames leaped everywhere and smoke rolled out through the door. A figure loomed up in the opening, heading inside that inferno, and Nacho lunged forward to grab the man. As he did so, Cambridge appeared from the other side and latched on to that arm, and Nacho saw that not surprisingly they had hold of Jake Maxwell.

"Le' go of me!" Maxwell shouted thickly. "Sandy's in there!"

"If she is you can't help her!" Cambridge told him, trying to pull Maxwell back away from the hellish heat that was coming from the store. Nacho added his efforts, but Maxwell was out of his head and had more than his normal strength. It took both of the West Texans several long moments to wrestle him away from the door and across the porch to the steps. Nacho slipped and fell when he reached the edge, but he hung on tightly to Maxwell and took both of the others with him when he went down.

The three of them sprawled in the dirt in front of the store. Nacho pushed himself up on an elbow and looked around. All the outlaws seemed to be gone, even the ones who had been wounded in the battle. The horses that had been tied up at the hitch rack had pulled loose and run off during the fighting, and so had the wagon team. Nacho spotted them standing about fifty yards down the road. There was no sign of anyone or anything else.

With a crash that sent sparks spiraling high into the night sky, the roof of the trading post collapsed. Most of the smoke went straight up now, instead of coming through the door, so visibility in the yard in front of the store improved rapidly as Nacho and Cambridge climbed painfully to their feet. Maxwell only made it as far as his knees. He stayed in that position, staring in disbelief at the blazing building. Grief and shock were etched on his features.

There was a bloody streak on Cambridge's face where a bullet or a splinter had grazed him. He looked over at Nacho and asked, "Are you all right?"

Nacho nodded. "They didn't hit me. What about Jake?"

Maxwell had a bloodstain on the right leg of his pants, high on the thigh. "Just a crease, I imagine," Cambridge said, looking at the stain that appeared black in the harsh glare of the light from the fire. "We'd better get him back to the station and have a look at it when we get the chance. Right now, though, we've got to make sure that fire doesn't spread."

"But what about the people inside?"

Cambridge shook his head. "There's no chance for them. The place went up too fast." He put a hand on Maxwell's shoulder. "You stay with Jake to make sure he doesn't do anything foolish. I'll get the bucket from the well and start wetting down the area around the building."

Nacho did as Cambridge told him, even though he didn't think Maxwell was likely to go charging back in there. The frenzy that had gripped the man earlier seemed to have passed now, leaving him in a state of shock. From the looks of him, he wasn't even going to be moving any time soon.

Cambridge hurried to the station well and came back with a bucket of water. He splashed it on several places where the fire was trying to spread away from the building. Luckily, the traffic around the trading post had beaten the grass down until there wasn't much left. It wouldn't be difficult to contain the blaze. However, the trading post was a total loss. As the flames died down, it was an almost unrecognizable heap of rubble.

Suddenly, Cambridge stopped what he was doing and let the water bucket hang in his left hand while he palmed out his Colt with the right. Several figures came staggering toward him out of the shadows, coughing and hanging on to each other for support. Nacho saw them, too, and he reached down to grab Maxwell's shoulder. "Jake, look!" he said urgently. "It's Sandra!"

Sandra Maxwell was indeed leading the grimy, bedraggled group.

With her were three men and another woman, no doubt the customers who had been in the store when the outlaws' raid began. Somehow, they had all miraculously survived the shooting and the fire.

But there was no sign of Theodore.

His glassy eyes finally blinking in amazement, Jake Maxwell realized what he was seeing as he stared at the little group, and he came up onto his feet quickly. Breaking into a run, he called, "Sandy!", and when he reached her, he grabbed her and pulled her into a tight embrace.

Nacho followed at a slower pace and came up to the group of survivors as Cambridge was asking, "What the devil happened in there? How did all of you get out?"

"It was the devil's own luck, mister," one of the men replied in a voice roughened by the smoke he had breathed before escaping from the store. "The way them outlaws was shootin', they could've killed us all. And then when that big 'un slung the lamp over and started the place on fire, I thought we was goners for sure."

"Miz Maxwell did it," the other woman said. "She's the one who led us through the smoke to the back door and got us out. We'd be in there right now with poor Mister Maxwell if she hadn't."

"Theodore didn't get away?" Cambridge asked sharply.

"Never had a chance," one of the other men replied. "He was dead 'fore the fire started. The leader of the gang emptied his Colt right into Maxwell's chest. Shot him to ribbons, he did."

Cambridge glanced over at Nacho and then asked the man, "Did they steal anything?"

"Didn't have a chance to. Y'all started shootin' outside, and then the fire started. I reckon all those ol' boys wanted to do then was get away."

Nacho could tell that Cambridge's mind was working rapidly from the intense look on the attorney's face. Cambridge holstered his gun and said, "If you feel up to it, why don't you men take over here and make sure that fire doesn't get out? We'll take Jake and Sandra back over to the stage station."

The survivors—two cowhands and a farmer and his wife—were willing to assume responsibility for the chore of keeping the fire contained. Besides, both Cambridge and Nacho knew that some of the other settlers in the area would probably be arriving in minutes. A fire of this size lit up the night sky for miles around, and folks always hurried to the scene of such tragedies to see if they could help.

"Come on, Jake," Cambridge said gently. "Let's get Sandra back to the station so that she can sit down."

Maxwell nodded and steered Sandra over to the station, his arm remaining around her shoulders. She leaned heavily against him, still coughing from time to time. Obviously, she had swallowed a lot of smoke before getting out of the burning building.

Nacho hurried ahead and lit the lamp again, then poured a cup of coffee for Sandra. He hesitated, then took a jug of corn liquor out of the cabinet where Maxwell kept it and splashed some of the moonshine into the cup, too. Sandra would likely need the fortification.

Maxwell led her in, got her to sit at the table, and gave her the cup. Sandra managed to swallow some of the strong black brew. Maxwell stayed right beside her, hovering over her. It was obvious now to Nacho that Maxwell was in love with her, whether she was his daughter-in-law or not. She was Maxwell's widowed daughter-in-law now, Nacho realized.

He went over to the stationkeeper and touched his shoulder. "I'm sorry, Jake," he said quietly, "about the trading post and about . . . Theodore."

Maxwell just shook his head and didn't say anything except to mutter, "Thanks, Nacho."

Cambridge tugged on Nacho's sleeve. "Come on. We've got to talk about this."

Nacho nodded in agreement. Despite his comment earlier about heavy thinking making his head hurt, he had been turning over the events of the evening in his mind, too, and he had reached some conclusions that he could hardly believe. He wanted to see what Cambridge had to say about it.

They stepped outside the door, leaving Maxwell and Sandra alone inside the station. Cambridge looked at the smoldering ruins of the trading post and shook his head. "I never thought this would happen," he said tiredly. "We've lost our lead to the gang now."

"But why would they raid the trading post?" Nacho asked. "Theodore was one of them."

"He was working for them. I reckon they didn't really consider him a member of the gang." Cambridge rubbed at his jaw and frowned in thought. "The way I see it, they must have decided they didn't need his help anymore, so they decided to hit the trading post and get what they could out of it."

Nacho objected, "But that man who was inside, he said they did not steal anything."

"I know. That's what's so strange about the whole thing. From the sound of it, the real reason they came was to kill Theodore Maxwell. The destruction was just incidental. But why in blazes would they want to do that? Unless, like I said, they'd decided not to work with him anymore and thought he might be a risk in the future."

"He was a risk right now," Nacho said flatly.

"You mean the trap we were setting? Of course he was, but the rest of the gang didn't know that. Only four of us even knew that Theodore had any connection with the outlaws."

Nacho didn't say anything. He took a deep breath, all the facts finally settling into place in his brain. He knew exactly why Theodore Maxwell had been killed, why the gang had risked coming out in the open for this raid. He even knew who the boss outlaw was now.

"Wait a minute," Cambridge said as Nacho turned away and started around the building toward the barn and the corrals. "Where are you going?"

"I got something to do," Nacho said, pausing but not looking back.

"There's nothing else we can do tonight except wait for the sheriff to show up and tell him what happened. Then we'll pay another visit to Seamus O'Shea. He's gone too far this time."

"No." Nacho finally turned so that his eyes met Cambridge's. "You're the smartest man I know, Billy, and I reckon I'm about the dumbest, but you're wrong this time. O'Shea doesn't have anything to do with those outlaws."

"What are you talking about?" Cambridge demanded, impatiently.

Nacho didn't answer. He was heading for the corral again. Cambridge didn't follow him, and Nacho knew that the lawyer was angry with him. Well, Billy had a right to be angry, Nacho thought. Cambridge had no idea just how much right he did have to be mad. But he was going to find out before this night was over.

Nacho threw a saddle on the horse he had been using and swung up onto its back. He guided it around the building and heeled it into a run as he reached the road. Cambridge was still standing in front of the station, and he had been joined now by Maxwell and Sandra. They all stared after Nacho as he rode away into the night.

He was headed south, toward the cutoff and the road that led to the Sand Ridge Baptist Church.

Chapter Fourteen

As he rode through the night, Nacho supposed he should have told Cambridge about his suspicions. No, they were more than suspicions, he decided. As far as he was concerned, they were iron-clad certainties. But it had been his own foolishness that was indirectly responsible for tonight's violence, and he was going to put things right himself. Besides, Cambridge wouldn't have believed him.

Nobody in his right mind would have.

Nacho didn't encounter anyone on the south road, and when he swung east onto the smaller trail, it seemed deserted, too. He urged the horse to greater speed, anxious to get this over with.

A three-quarter autumn moon gave plenty of light to ride by, and Nacho was able to make good time. Soon he could see moonlight reflecting from the whitewashed steeple of the church up ahead. He pulled his horse back to a walk and slipped his Colt from its holster. The hammer was resting on an empty chamber, as was Nacho's habit, but now he opened the loading gate, rotated the cylinder, and filled that chamber with one of the cartridges from his belt loops. He was about to go up against the trickiest son-of-a-bitch he had ever encountered, and he wanted the gun fully loaded. He eased the weapon back into the holster as he entered the little yard in front of the church.

A dim light was burning in one of the building's rear windows, behind the sanctuary. There was no parsonage, so Nacho assumed that the Reverend John Livingston had his living quarters back there. He dismounted and tied his horse to the hitch rack, then went to the front doors of the church and rapped sharply on one of them. When there was no response after a minute, he knocked again, louder this time.

After a moment, he heard footsteps on the other side of the door. It swung open, and Livingston peered out at him, a puzzled look on the preacher's face. Livingston was carrying a candle in one hand and a Bible in the other, a finger stuck between the pages to mark his place. He had removed his coat and tie but still wore his shirt and the pants of his dark suit.

"Mr. Graves . . . Nacho," Livingston said. "What are you doing here?"

"I came to see you, Reverend. Sorry to bother you this late, but it's mighty important."

Livingston stepped back. "Well, come in, come in. You didn't have to knock. The doors of the church are never locked. We're always open for prayer and meditation."

"This is going to take more than prayer, Reverend," Nacho said as he entered the church. He glanced up at the cross above the altar and the pictures of Jesus that were hung on the walls of the little foyer. A distinct feeling of unease rippled through him. If he was wrong, would what he was about to do border on the sacrilegious?

He put those thoughts out of his head as Livingston smiled and said, "Nothing is beyond the power of prayer, my friend. Come with me."

Livingston put his Bible under his arm and rested his hand on Nacho's shoulder as the two men walked down the aisle toward the front of the sanctuary. This was the first time Nacho had been inside the church, and he saw that it looked like most of the other Baptist churches he had seen— stained glass windows, rough pews with no padding, a slightly raised pulpit. It was nowhere nearly as elaborate as the missions where he had been taken as a boy, but Nacho sensed some of the same majesty and sense of purpose about the place. The people who came here to worship were honest and simple . . . good people who deserved better than they had gotten.

When they reached the front row, Livingston gestured toward the long pew and said, "Why don't you have a seat?"

Nacho shook his head. "I'd rather stand."

"All right." The minister smiled again. "How can I help you, brother?"

Nacho drew the Colt smoothly and quickly and lined it on Livingston's belly. "You can drop the act and admit you are the most lowdown outlaw skunk who ever walked the earth," he said in a cold voice.

Livingston's eyes widened in alarm. "Lord help us," he murmured. "Whatever in the world are you talking about, Brother Graves?"

Nacho shook his head. "I'm not your brother. I know all about you now, Livingston. I know you're really the leader of that outlaw gang. Theodore Maxwell probably could have told us that—but he's dead now. Your henchmen murdered him tonight. They burned down the trading post and nearly killed five other people. I think you will hang for what they have done."

Staring at him in disbelief, Livingston said, "You've lost your mind, Nacho. I don't have the slightest idea what you're talking about, but I'd like to help you." He started to lift his arm and reach out to Nacho.

The *vaquero* stepped back quickly, keeping the gun steady in its aim. "Don't try anything, Livingston," he snapped. "I want to take you alive, but I'll put a bullet through your knee if you try to get away."

Livingston took a deep breath, putting an expression of pity on his face. "I'm sorry you're having these delusions. What can I say to convince you that you're wrong?"

"Nothing," Nacho said flatly. "You see, I know you're the boss, Livingston. You ordered that raid on the trading post and told Graham to make sure Theodore Maxwell died. You did that because I was foolish enough earlier today to tell you that we knew Theodore was working with the gang. You were the only one who knew besides me and Billy, and Jake and Sandra Maxwell. It had to be you."

Livingston sighed and shook his head. "I wish I could make you see that you're mistaken." He opened his Bible and went on, "But since I can't . . ."

Nacho saw the little pistol in Livingston's hand, saw the barrel tipping up toward him. At the same instant, he heard the soft footsteps behind him. Torn between two potential threats, he twisted to the side, trying to get out of the line of fire.

Something crashed against his head, sending him reeling. He heard the spiteful report of Livingston's pistol and felt a white-hot lance of pain in his right arm. His own gun slipped from his fingers as he staggered and fell. Something warm and wet trickled down across his face from his scalp, and his right arm was rapidly going numb. He tried to push himself back up.

A kick slammed into his side, knocking him sprawling in front of the pews again. He looked up and saw Livingston looming above him. All traces of Christian charity and compassion were gone from the preacher's face now. They had been replaced by a look of pure evil and hatred.

Another face swam into view in the circle of yellow light cast by the candle in Livingston's hand. Nacho saw the carbine she held and knew she had hit him with the butt of it. She was the only one who could have moved up behind him that quietly.

"We've got to get rid of him," he heard Dove O'Shea say with an unmistakable tone of command in her voice.

The darkness took him then, and at that moment, he didn't much care.

The fire was out, the trading post in ruins. Jake Maxwell looked at the pile of blackened rubble in the moonlight and shook his head. A big part of his life had gone up in flames tonight—the business he had started so many years earlier . . . and the son who had somehow gone horribly wrong. Cambridge felt deep sympathy for his old friend as he stood beside Maxwell and Sandra.

"We'll rebuild it," Maxwell said abruptly, his arm tightening around Sandra's shoulders. "No reason the store can't be better than ever. I'll keep runnin' the station, and you can handle the tradin' post, Sandy. I reckon you been doin' most of the work there lately anyway, what with Theodore's bein' busy with his owlhoot pards."

Cambridge heard the bitterness in Maxwell's voice as he spoke about his son. "You don't mean that, Jake," he said softly. "Theodore did wrong, but he was still your son. You'll regret it if you don't grieve for him."

"What do you think I been doin' these last few months, Billy?" Maxwell lifted a hand and wearily rubbed his face. "Reckon you're right, though. But I'll have to see to it later. Right now there's other things to do. Like figurin' out where Nacho took off to in such a hurry."

"He was upset about *something*, that's for sure. Before he left, he said I was wrong about Seamus O'Shea being the leader of that gang. He acted like he thought he knew who was really in charge. But he didn't say anything else, just rode off like the devil was after him."

"Speakin' of the devil, I wonder where the preacher is," Maxwell said. "He usually shows up any time there's trouble, wantin' to help folks."

Cambridge frowned. Maxwell was right. People from all around had converged on the fire, even though it had been mostly out by the time they showed up. The neighbors had gone on their way now, after promising that they would be back in the morning to help Maxwell any way they could. But Reverend Livingston hadn't put in an appearance, and even though Cambridge hadn't known the minister for long, he agreed with Maxwell that his absence was unusual.

"I suppose he might not have heard about the fire," Cambridge mused. "Either that, or he was busy with something else."

"Reckon so." Maxwell had a look of deep concentration on his face. Suddenly, he turned to Sandra and asked, "You recollect that man and woman who came to the tradin' post a few nights ago and talked to Theodore?"

She nodded. "I remember them. We never did figure out who they were."

"Well, talkin' about Reverend Livingston just now got me to thinkin'. He drives a buggy just like the one that came here that night."

"Wait a minute," Cambridge said. "What are you two talking about?"

Quickly, Maxwell told the lawyer about the arrival in the middle of the night of a buggy carrying two mysterious figures. "Ever since we found out Theodore was mixed up with them outlaws, I been thinkin' maybe those folks were part of the gang, too," Maxwell said. "But they couldn't have been, because now that I think about it, I'm almost sure that was the preacher's buggy."

Cambridge's frown deepened and he gave a little shake of his head. The ideas that were suddenly popping up in his brain, prompted by what Maxwell and Sandra had just said, were too crazy to be true. And yet . . .

Nacho had been talking to Livingston earlier that day, while Cambridge was inside the store laying out the bait for Theodore. Could Nacho have said anything to Livingston about their plans? It was possible, Cambridge decided. After all, Nacho would be likely to trust a man of the cloth. Raised in West Texas with its mixture of white and Spanish cultures, Nacho might give a Baptist preacher the same regard and admiration—and trust—that he would a priest.

But even Cambridge had a hard time believing that somebody like John Livingston could be the secret leader of a bloodthirsty band of outlaws.

But still, Nacho had taken the south road, and that was the route that would ultimately take him to the church. . . .

"Reckon I'd better do some riding, too," he announced. "Sorry to have to leave you right now, Jake, but I've got to check on something."

Maxwell and Sandra both looked baffled, but the stationkeeper said, "Sure, Billy. Whatever you want. Help yourself to a horse."

Cambridge went back into the station and got his hat, then saddled the same mount he had been using. He didn't like keeping Maxwell in the dark, but if he had explained the nebulous theory that his brain had put together, Jake would have thought he had lost his mind for sure. Better to prove it one way or the other first.

Of course, if he was wrong, then he had no idea where Nacho had gotten off to or what sort of trouble the ranch foreman had found for himself.

Maxwell and Sandra were standing in front of the station as Cambridge galloped off. He gave them a wave, which Maxwell returned. The two of them looked good somehow, standing side by side like that, drawing strength from each other. He didn't know what had happened between them in the past—didn't really want to know, to be truthful about it—but he had a feeling that when a suitable interval had passed, Sandra would marry another Maxwell. The right Maxwell this time. And if that happened, Cambridge would wish them both all the luck and happiness in the world.

Right now, though, he had to find Nacho.

When he reached the cutoff, he swung east, heading toward the church. Nacho had a good half-hour's start on him, so Cambridge urged his horse on at top speed, hoping to cut down that lead. Knowing Nacho, he was probably in some sort of trouble by now.

Cambridge didn't slow down until he came within sight of the church. Then he pulled his horse back to a walk and studied the place in the moonlight as he approached. The whitewashed building was dark, no lights showing anywhere. And there were no horses tied up in front, either, no sign of the animal Nacho had ridden away from the stage station.

Just because he wasn't here now didn't mean he hadn't been here, Cambridge reasoned. He reined in and swung down from the saddle, flipping the lines over the hitch rack with a practiced twist. The front doors of the church probably weren't locked, but Cambridge knocked anyway, not wanting to walk in unannounced and frighten Livingston.

There was no answer, so Cambridge called, "Reverend? Reverend Livingston? It's Billy Cambridge." When there was still no reply, he reached out with his left hand and took hold of the knob on the right-side door. It turned in his grip. He shoved the panel open as he slid his Colt from its holster and stepped back.

The interior of the church was dark and silent. Cambridge hesitated for a long moment, not liking the fact that he would make a good target when he went inside and was silhouetted against the moonlight in the opening. But he wouldn't find out anything standing around here. He moved through the entrance quickly, stepping to one side as soon as he was in.

He listened intently for a footstep, the sound of breathing . . . the click of a gun hammer being drawn back . . . anything. Instead there was nothing. The church was as quiet as a tomb.

Taking a chance, Cambridge called again, "Reverend Livingston!" He crouched as soon as the words were out of his mouth, reaching out with his free hand to steady himself against one of the rear pews.

After waiting for several minutes that seemed even longer, Cambridge stood up again, satisfied that he was alone in the church. Moving slowly, feeling his way along, he went up the aisle toward the pulpit, and when he got there, he reached into his pocket for a match. With a rasping noise that sounded even louder in the utter silence, he scraped it into life, closing his eyes first so that the glare wouldn't blind him.

When he opened them again a few seconds later, blinking against the harsh light, he looked around and saw that he was alone, just as he had thought. Spotting a row of candles in a plain brass holder on one end of the pulpit, he went over and began to light them. The illumination grew until he could see even into the corners of the big, high-ceilinged room.

There were some other rooms in the back of the building, probably where Livingston slept, and he would have to check all of them. But first he wanted to take a good look around the sanctuary. That didn't take long. Nothing seemed to be disturbed. There were hymnals lying on the pews, and a small vase of flowers sat at the other end of the pulpit from the candles. None of the pews were toppled over or even knocked out of arrangement. From the looks of things, the place was ready for Sunday services.

Which were scheduled to start in about twelve hours, Cambridge thought. Livingston should have been here, praying or working on his sermon or whatever it was preachers did on a Saturday night. With his gun still held ready in his hand, Cambridge hurriedly went through the other rooms. He found Livingston's bunk and some of the minister's clothes in one of the small chambers, but no sign of the minister himself.

Cambridge felt in his bones that Nacho had come here to accuse Livingston of being the head of the outlaw gang. Maybe Nacho had dragged

Livingston out of the church and taken him at gunpoint to Sherman, intending to turn him over to the sheriff. That was possible, but not likely. Nacho would have probably brought Livingston back to the stage station and let Cambridge handle things from there. Assuming, of course, that Livingston was indeed guilty—and that was a hell of an assumption, Cambridge thought.

He holstered his gun and cuffed back his hat, sighing as he pondered what to do next. Suddenly, as he stared down at the floor, he spotted something he hadn't noticed before. There were a couple of small stains of some kind on one of the planks.

Cambridge went down on one knee and reached out to touch the spots. His finger came away slightly sticky, and when he held it up, he saw that the tip had a reddish-brown cast to it now. His face settling into grim lines, he muttered, "Nacho . . ."

The spots were blood, sure enough.

By the time Cambridge got back to the stagecoach station, Sandra was already lying down in Maxwell's room. The stationkeeper was sitting at the long table in the main room, nursing a cup of coffee. As Cambridge came in, Maxwell looked up and said, "Howdy, Billy. You find Nacho?"

"Not yet," Cambridge replied, a bleak look in his eyes. "I'm afraid there's more trouble, Jake."

Maxwell sighed. "No end to it, is there? What is it now? You want me to fetch Sandra to hear about it, too?"

Cambridge shook his head and said, "If she's resting, then leave her alone. She's been through enough the last few days."

"That's the damned truth," Maxwell muttered.

"And so have you, Jake. I'm sorry as hell Nacho and I came here and helped bring all this down on your head."

"You didn't do no such thing," Maxwell declared. "It was Theodore's doin', plain and simple. You boys pokin' around may've stirred things up a mite sooner than they would've been otherwise, but it would've all come out sooner or later. I'm just thankful there wasn't anybody else killed."

Cambridge nodded and sat down across the table from his old friend. "I think Nacho went after the leader of the outlaws," he said.

"O'Shea?" Maxwell started to shake his head.

Cambridge stopped him by saying crisply, "Not O'Shea. The ringleader of the gang is John Livingston."

For a couple of seconds, Maxwell didn't say anything. Then, eyes wide with surprise, he exclaimed, "The preacher?"

"That's right." Cambridge had thought it all out during the ride back from the church, and he was convinced now that Livingston was behind all the deviltry. In a firm voice, he explained to Maxwell how Nacho might have revealed the plot to catch the outlaws to Livingston earlier that day.

"But you don't know for sure he did that," Maxwell pointed out.

"Nacho was certain he had the gang leader's identity figured out. He flat out told me it wasn't O'Shea, and he headed south, not west into the breaks. The only person he knows anywhere in that direction, at least around here, is Livingston."

Maxwell still looked doubtful. "Those owlhoots chased you and Nacho the other day when you were with the preacher and that O'Shea girl. Would they have done that if Livingston was their boss?"

"They might have if they were trying to scare us off. None of their bullets came really close, and they backed off in a hurry when Nacho and I put up a fight. Anyway, what better way to turn aside suspicion than to seem a victim yourself?"

"Reckon that makes sense," Maxwell said, rubbing his beard-stubbled jaw. "Hard to believe a preacher would be up to such mischief, though."

"Livingston mentioned, too, that he'd only been in these parts for a few months. Did he show up about the same time all the trouble started?"

"Come to think of it, he did. The Baptists had been without a preacher or even a circuit rider for a while when Livingston drove up and told folks he'd been called to take over the church. Reckon it didn't occur to nobody to challenge him on it. Folks were just glad to have a preacher around again." Maxwell sounded like he was starting to believe Cambridge's theory.

"I just got back from the church," the lawyer continued grimly. "Livingston's not there. Nobody is. But there's blood on the floor. I figure there was a fight."

"Nacho went there and told Livingston what he'd figured out," Maxwell guessed.

"That's the way I see it. He probably intended to bring Livingston back here. But Livingston put up a struggle and somebody got hurt. It must have been Nacho, or they would have turned up by now."

"Lordy," Maxwell breathed. "When I said there was no end to it, I didn't figure it'd get this tangled up. What do we do now?"

161

Cambridge stood up. "I have to hope that Nacho is still alive. If he is, Livingston probably took him to the gang's hide-out, somewhere over there in the breaks. Reckon he'd want to know whether or not Nacho had told anybody else what he'd figured out."

"Then you're left with tryin' to find the gang's hide-out, which ain't goin' to be easy." Maxwell's voice hardened. "Not in time, anyway."

"That's why I need your help, Jake."

Maxwell stood up, too, and faced Cambridge across the table. "Anything I can do, Billy, you know that," he said solemnly.

"I want you to take me to Seamus O'Shea."

The stationkeeper looked puzzled. "What makes you think goin' to see O'Shea would do any good? I thought you said you figured he didn't have any part in this after all."

"I don't, but he probably knows that part of the country better than anybody. I had a feeling right from the first that he might have an idea where those outlaws are holing up. I'm counting on you and me being able to talk him into helping us." Cambridge shrugged. "For one thing, his daughter seems to have been taken in by Livingston's act, too. O'Shea might not like knowing that Dove had been fooled like that."

"Don't reckon he'd care for the idea, now that you mention it." Maxwell nodded. "I'm with you, Billy. You intend to start tonight?"

"There's no time to wait for morning."

"Well, between the two of us, we ought to be able to find O'Shea's place. I've been there once, bought some horses from him. And you and Nacho paid him a visit a few days ago."

"We'll find him," Cambridge said firmly, not allowing a trace of doubt to creep into his voice. "And he'll help us."

Cambridge just wished he felt as sure as he sounded.

Chapter Fifteen

Somebody was using a hammer and tongs on Nacho's skull, trying to shape it into a horseshoe. That's what it felt like, anyway, when consciousness began to seep back into him. Gradually, he realized it was his own pulse that was sending the pounding jolts of pain through his head, every time it beat.

The fact that he was hanging head down, tied over a saddle, his belly rubbed about raw by the unfamiliar position, didn't help matters any. The horse plodded along as Nacho tried to pry his eyes open. He had already discovered that his wrists were tied tightly to his ankles by a cord that passed under the animal's belly. Opening his eyes and lifting his head were about the only maneuvers he could accomplish in his present condition.

Everything was still dark when he finally got his eyes open. No, not everything, he realized a moment later. He could see a few vague shapes moving past and guessed they were trees and bushes. It was still night, even darker than when he had last been awake. The moon had set by now, leaving nothing but faint starlight filtering down from the heavens.

The longer he stayed conscious, the more memories came back to him. Might have been better to remain out cold, he thought. At least that way, he hadn't been forced to think about how Dove O'Shea had played him for a fool. *The best judge of women in West Texas . . .* that was a laugh.

For as long as he lived—which probably wouldn't be very long, he thought bitterly—he would never forget the scornful look on her face as she had gazed down at him there in the church. She and Livingston had both been in on it all along. In fact, the way she had given orders, *she* was probably the boss, not the preacher.

Like father, like daughter, Nacho supposed. Dove was living up to both sides of her heritage, the Comanche . . . and the Comanchero.

From the sound of the hoofbeats, there were two other horses on the trail. Dove's and Livingston's, he supposed. So far, they didn't seem to have noticed that he was awake. If he could somehow get loose, he could slip away into the night—

No chance of that. The knots on his wrists and ankles were too tight. Dove knew what she was doing. He felt confident that she had been the one who tied him onto the horse.

He let his head hang loosely from his shoulders and spent a few minutes cursing himself. He had been taken in completely by Dove's demure pose. The real Dove was the one in buckskins who had pointed that carbine at him and Cambridge and threatened to use it. Nacho could see that now, now that it was too late to do him any good.

And Livingston had fooled him, too. Even after he had figured out that the preacher was part of the gang, he hadn't expected Livingston to reach into a Bible and come up with a gun. The book had been hollowed out so that a little pistol could be hidden in it. An old trick, but it worked.

He was a little surprised to still be alive. They probably wanted to take him out well away from the church before they killed him. They might even be heading for the gang's hide-out. Maybe he'd finally find out where it was, not that it mattered now.

Somewhere along the way, Nacho lost consciousness again. He drifted in and out of oblivion, not aware of anything much except the pain in his head and the steady gait of the horse. After what seemed like an eternity had passed, the sound of voices finally dragged him back from the haven of darkness.

". . . get in deeper an' deeper," a deep voice was rumbling. "I'm dead set agin' this, girl."

The gravelly tones were familiar somehow to Nacho, and after a moment he placed them. The voice belonged to Seamus O'Shea, the former Comanchero.

"I been hearin' things about what you been doin', an' I don't like it,"

O'Shea went on. "Give it up, Dove, an' light out now 'fore it gets any worse."

She just laughed, a harsh, strident sound. "You're a fine one to talk, old man," she snapped. "You rode with some of the worst bandits in the world for two years, and now you have the gall to tell me to be a good girl."

"That was different. I was out o' my head with grievin' for your mama." O'Shea sighed. "This is plain viciousness."

"We're just protecting ourselves." That was Livingston. "You can understand that, Mr. O'Shea. We can't let Graves live. We just have to find out what he's told that lawyer friend of his before we kill him."

Well, that was a little bit encouraging, Nacho thought. Every hour he stayed alive was another hour when he might have a chance to get away. He didn't hold out much hope of being rescued. Billy wouldn't know where to look for him, wouldn't have any idea that Livingston was even mixed up in all this.

"I'm tired of arguing," Dove said angrily. "Just watch our back trail, Pa. If anybody comes along, you've got your choice. You can turn them back—or kill them."

With that, the horses started moving again. Nacho turned his head a little and opened his eyes, wincing as the dawn light struck them. The three of them were passing in front of O'Shea's cabin, and the old frontiersman was standing there with a Sharps in his hands, glowering after his daughter and the phony preacher. Even upside down, Nacho could see the concern on the man's face, and he also saw the way O'Shea's eyes widened in surprise when he noticed that Nacho was awake. But the former Comanchero's lips clamped tightly together, and he didn't say anything.

If Nacho was waiting for O'Shea to help him, it was a futile hope. O'Shea just stood there, watching, until the little procession vanished into the woods.

Sunrise found Cambridge and Maxwell on the rough, almost invisible track that passed for a trail in this part of the country. They weren't following the exact same route that Cambridge and Nacho had taken on their only visit to Seamus O'Shea's cabin, but Maxwell assured the attorney that this way was a little faster.

"Ought to sight his smoke soon," Maxwell said when they paused momentarily to rest the horses. "I imagine Seamus is an early riser. He'll have breakfast cookin' by now." He took off his hat and massaged his temples in weariness. It had been a long night for both men.

Cambridge had hated to drag Maxwell away from the station. The man had had enough trouble in his own life lately. When they had roused Sandra and explained the situation to her, however, she had insisted that Maxwell do everything he could to help Cambridge find Nacho.

"Nothing you can do here will bring back Theodore . . . the way he used to be," she had said softly. "I'll be all right, Jake, really. You go on."

There was nothing Maxwell could do about the trading post, either, not right away. Rebuilding it would be a long process. But rebuild it he would; Cambridge was sure of that. There was a new light of determination in Maxwell's eyes whenever he spoke of the future. So maybe some good would come out of this mess after all. Cambridge hoped so.

They pushed on, and less than an hour later, Maxwell spotted the smoke from O'Shea's chimney, just as he had predicted. A few more minutes brought them in sight of the ramshackle cabin.

Cambridge reined in. "Do we just ride up there, or is he liable to take a shot at us if we do?"

"As long as we sing out before we get there, I don't reckon Seamus'll start blastin'," Maxwell replied with a tired grin. "Come on." He heeled his horse into motion.

A minute later, as they started down the hill toward the cabin, Maxwell called, "Hello the cabin! Seamus! Seamus O'Shea! It's me, Jake Maxwell!"

There was no response. Cambridge and Maxwell looked at each other, shrugged, and kept riding.

The shot shattered the early morning stillness.

Cambridge and Maxwell both left their saddles, diving in opposite directions as the slug whined over their heads. Rolling as he landed, Cambridge came up in a crouch, the Colt in his hand. He'd had a glimpse of muzzle flash, somewhere off to the right of the cabin. O'Shea had to be hidden in the woods over there. Holding his fire, Cambridge scurried behind a tree and waited. A few yards away, Maxwell was doing the same thing.

Another shot echoed through the trees, but it didn't come anywhere close to them. Maxwell got to his feet, leaned against the trunk of the tree he was using for cover, and shouted, "Hold on, Seamus! No need for shootin'! We're just here to talk!"

"Go home!" O'Shea called from his concealment. "Get th' hell out o' th' breaks an' don't come back!"

Maxwell looked over at Cambridge and shook his head. O'Shea's violent reaction to their visit didn't make any more sense to him than it did to the lawyer.

"Listen, O'Shea! This is Billy Cambridge. My friend and I were out here the other day. We need your help!"

"I ain't helpin' nobody! Now be on your way, or I ain't goin' t' be responsible for what happens!"

Cambridge called over to Maxwell, too quietly for O'Shea to hear, "We're going to have to flush him out of there. Whether he's willing to help us find that hide-out or not, we can't let him keep us pinned down here."

Maxwell nodded and motioned with the Winchester he had taken with him when he leaped off his horse. Cambridge understood. He pointed up, indicating for Maxwell to aim high.

As Maxwell poked the muzzle of the rifle around the tree and started blazing away as fast as he could work the lever, Cambridge darted out from his own cover and raced for another clump of trees some thirty feet away. The growth was thicker there, and he would be able to work his way around to the side of O'Shea without exposing himself very often or for too long at a time. Of course, O'Shea could still get lucky and nail him, but that was a chance Cambridge had to take.

This wasn't the first time Cambridge and Maxwell had worked together in such a situation. When they were both in the Texas Rangers, they had fought outlaws and Indians and Mexican troops. But a lot of years had passed since those days, years that Billy Cambridge had spent for the most part in courtrooms, risking nothing more dangerous than an ornery jurist's displeasure. The instincts were still all there, though, and still working just fine. He spent the next fifteen minutes moving into position. O'Shea sent a couple of shots his direction, but the bullets went wild. The old Comanchero didn't know exactly where he was, Cambridge decided.

That was what he thought until he darted out from a clump of brush, heading for the next piece of cover, and found his feet kicked out from under him. He went down hard, trying to twist and bring his revolver into play. A booted foot hit his wrist, knocking the gun away, then came down hard on his chest.

The muzzle of a Sharps centered itself on Cambridge's nose from less than a foot away. Seamus O'Shea towered over him, his face dark and thunderous, eyes narrowed and shining with a murderous gleam. At this range, when the Sharps went off it wouldn't leave a hell of a lot of Cambridge's head intact.

Cambridge made his mouth work. "Reckon I was wrong about you," he said.

O'Shea tilted his head slightly to one side. "What you mean by that?"

"I guess you're still an outlaw after all."

Something changed in O'Shea's eyes then. The gleam fled, to be replaced by a look of more sadness than Cambridge had ever seen. O'Shea moved the barrel of the carbine away from Cambridge's face and took the foot off his chest. "Why the hell didn't you an' that Meskin go back t' West Texas where you belong?" he muttered.

"Drop the gun, Seamus!" Maxwell shouted from twenty feet away, lining the Winchester's sights on the burly old frontiersman.

Cambridge held up a hand as he hurriedly pulled himself into a sitting position, knowing somehow that O'Shea was no longer a threat. "Wait a minute, Jake!" he called. "It's all right."

"Th' hell it is," O'Shea growled. He canted the barrel of the rifle over his shoulder and shook his head. "Ain't nothin' ever goin' t' be right again. But come on back t' th' house, an' we'll talk about it."

"What the hell you got here?" Fingers tangled in Nacho's hair and brutally jerked his head up as he hung helplessly from the horse.

He looked up into a face that was familiar, even though he hadn't seen it before except with a bandanna tied over the lower half. The outlaw was grinning down at him, obviously anticipating the pleasure of killing him.

"Let go of him, Graham," Dove said. "Cut him loose and get him down from there."

"Sure." Graham released Nacho's head and let it sag toward the ground again. He slipped a knife from his belt and bent over to cut the bonds holding the *vaquero*.

Nacho's hands and feet were numb from being tied over the horse's back for so long, and he couldn't stop himself as he fell loosely to the ground. The breath was jarred out of his lungs. He gasped for air, then winced as the blood began to flow back into his extremities.

Trying to take his mind off that and the pain in his side, he looked around. Without a doubt, this was where the outlaws had been hiding after they pulled their jobs. They were deep in the heavily wooded breaks, a good five miles past Seamus O'Shea's cabin. There was no trail leading here, and if a man wasn't extremely familiar with the landmarks in the area, he'd be hopelessly lost inside of ten minutes. Nacho had noticed a few things while trussed up, but he knew he couldn't hope to find his way out—or back in.

"Take him inside," Dove ordered. She and Livingston had dismounted.

She was wearing the buckskins now, Nacho saw as a couple of the outlaws grasped his arms and jerked him to his feet. She must have changed at her father's cabin, he decided, because he was almost sure she had been wearing a dress when she clouted him back at the church.

The cabin was a simple log structure with a plank porch. Nacho had no way of knowing if the gang had built it to use as a hide-out or if they had just taken over the building after somebody else abandoned it. The distinction didn't matter, of course; he could die here just as easily either way.

The two desperados dragged him into the main room of the cabin and dropped him on the floor. His legs still wouldn't support him. Dove and Livingston strolled into the shack. The preacher was wearing his dark jacket but hadn't bothered with the string tie. And the gunbelt strapped around his waist was another difference.

Nacho forced a grin onto his face and said, "I suppose your flock will have to hold services without you this morning, Reverend. It's Sunday, you know."

"I know," Livingston said. He chuckled. "I think those yokels can manage without me just this once. I want to watch you beg for your life before we kill you, Graves. Then I'll go back and spin some story about being called away to visit a dying man or some such drivel. Nobody will be any the wiser."

"And you'll go right on working with these *bandidos*."

"Of course. A preacher finds out all the secrets in a community, like who has money and who doesn't. After all, everybody trusts a man of God. You're proof of that."

"Stop gloating," Dove said. She came over to Nacho and knelt so that she could meet his eyes more easily. She slipped a knife from a sheath of soft buckskin at her waist. "I am Comanche. You know what that means, Nacho. You can die quickly and easily, or you can die long and in agony. But either way you will die. You must die. You know that."

"Because I know what you really are." His lips drew back in a grimace of contempt and disgust.

She reached out, put the tip of the knife against his cheek, and drew it down slowly, leaving a thin red line behind it. "Because you know what I am," she agreed. "Did you tell anyone else of John's involvement in our little enterprise?"

Nacho didn't say anything. They were going to torture him anyway, he figured, because they wouldn't believe his first answer, no matter what it was.

Graham slouched into the room, thumbs hooked in his gunbelt. "Hey, you're startin' without me," he protested.

"Shut up!" Dove snapped without taking her eyes off Nacho's. "What is it going to be? Do you talk and die quickly, or be stubborn and make this take all day?"

"Go to hell," Nacho said.

The tip of the blade dug deeper into his cheek.

Livingston grinned and said, "As the only minister present, I think such pronouncements are more in my line. Don't you?"

"I never thought I'd get her back, y'see," Seamus O'Shea said heavily as he sat down on the steps in front of his cabin. "After Dove's mama . . . died . . . an' I went with the Comancheros, she was raised by this preacher what was there at Fort Griffin. When I finally come back, th' preacher was gone, an' his wife an' his own young 'uns an' Dove with him." O'Shea gazed off into the woods, but he was obviously seeing something else. "Little Dove, that was her name. Purtiest little thing you ever saw. Th' picture of her mama, she was. She'd a had a grown-up name later, o' course, but—we never got around to it." He sighed. "Yep, I figgered she was gone for good. An' prob'ly better off for it. I had too much blood on m' hands. She didn't need me for a pappy."

"But she finally came back," Cambridge prodded, knowing they probably didn't have the time to listen to this story but also knowing that they would never get O'Shea's help otherwise.

"Couple year ago. Showed up out o' th' blue, she did. I knew her right away, though, even with all th' years that'd gone by. She still looks like her mama. An' there's that scar . . . you can't miss it."

Maxwell asked, "Did she say where she'd been or what she'd been doin' all that time?"

O'Shea shook his head. "Not right away. An' I didn't care, neither. I was just glad t' have her back again. Come t' find out, though, she'd stayed with that preacher fella an' his family when they left th' fort. When she was fourteen, she . . . she got him t' come t' her bed."

Cambridge and Maxwell waited, not knowing what to say as the ugly details of Dove's life story slowly emerged from her father.

"Well, th' two of 'em up an' left. Livingston deserted his own wife an' kids an' took up with Dove. He gave up preachin' th' gospel, 'cept when they was tryin' t' swindle somebody an' they needed him t' play that part. They did whatever they had t' do t' survive. I 'spect they even robbed an' killed some folks. Then they heard I'd settled here an' come t' pay me a visit. Dove showed up first t' get th' lay o' th' land, an' then here come Livingston a little later. When I found out what they'd been doin', I thought for a while 'bout killin' him, but then I decided that wouldn't be fair. It was *her*." O'Shea's big hands clenched into fists and trembled slightly. "*She* was th' one who done it all. He was just weak an' went along with her."

Maxwell put a hand on O'Shea's shoulder and said fervently, "God, I'm sorry, Seamus. It must've been hell for you."

"Nope. Worse'n that. I reckon I'll be goin' t' hell when my time comes, but I ain't scared. I've done seen worse."

"How did they round up that bunch of owlhoots to work with them?" Cambridge asked.

O'Shea shrugged his massive shoulders. "They'd run into most of 'em over the years in one robbers' roost or another. Dove worked in them places when she had to, you know, servicin' th' men. When her an' Livingston got th' idea o' startin' a gang here, they got in touch with a fella called Graham. He brought most o' th' others with him. Took a while t' set ever'thin' up, but once they did, it way payin' off mighty handsome."

"Until they held up that stage with Nacho and me on it," Cambridge said. "I'm sorry about everything you've been through, O'Shea, but I think they've captured my friend. I've got to find him before they kill him."

"They've got him, all right," O'Shea said. Cambridge stiffened.

"You've seen them?" the lawyer asked.

"Just before sun-up this mornin'. Dove an' Livingston stopped by on their way t' th' hide-out. They had th' Meskin with 'em, an' they wanted me t' stop anybody from trailin' 'em. That's what I was tryin' t' do when I took them potshots at you two."

"But you didn't want to kill us," Maxwell said.

"You've been a friend t' me, Jake, when most folks wouldn't be. An' there's been too much killin'. I've seen it all my life, an' I'm damn sick of it."

"Then help us stop them from murdering Nacho," Cambridge said. "It's time to put an end to this, O'Shea. Will you take us to the gang's hide-out?"

"How do y' figger I know where it is?"

Cambridge smiled, even though tension had his belly in a knot. "I don't think there's anything in these breaks that you don't know about."

"Well, I reckon that's true enough." O'Shea sighed and then stood up. "I'll take you there."

"O'Shea . . ." Cambridge put a hand on the man's arm. "I can't make you any promises about Dove."

The old Comanchero—maybe the *last* Comanchero alive anywhere— just looked at him and said, "It's too late for promises anyway."

Chapter Sixteen

When he was sixteen, a bronc he had been trying to gentle had thrown Nacho and stomped on him a few times, busting him up so that he had to spend three weeks in bed. That had hurt pretty bad. So far, what Dove had done to him hadn't been much worse than getting stomped by that bronc.

But Dove was just getting started.

His feet smeared with blood from the razor-thin slashes all over them, Nacho sagged against the ropes that held him to the chair. Dove had gone outside, taking Livingston with her, in an effort to curb her impatience and anger. If she let her temper run away with her, she might kill the prisoner too soon, before they found out what they wanted to know. That rage was the white side of her coming out, Nacho decided, trying to make some sense out of the fog of pain that had descended on his brain. The Comanche side wouldn't have any trouble staying cool and calm through the torture.

Graham was the only member of the gang inside the cabin at the moment. All the others had found excuses to go outside when Dove started working on Nacho with the knife. Now Graham stood in front of the captive and said, "Mister, you're crazy. You'd better give Dove what she wants, or she's liable to take until tomorrow to kill you."

Nacho managed to shake his head. "You should have killed me . . . when you had the chance . . . that day when you held up the stagecoach."

"Yeah, I should have. Reckon I felt grateful. It's not every day you run across twenty thousand dollars in one place."

"What did you do . . . with the money?"

"What *could* I do with it? You see any place to spend it in these woods? We've still got it cached under the floor, 'cept for a few hundred Dove and the preacher took for expense money. They've got to stay lookin' respectable, you know."

"Respectable," Nacho repeated bitterly. "I'll never tell them anything."

"Hell, then I'd be doin' you a favor if I put a bullet through your brain right now." Graham gave a snort of derisive laughter. "But then she might take that knife after me, and I wouldn't want that."

"Wouldn't want what?" Dove asked as she stepped in the door, Livingston following behind her.

Graham moved quickly away from Nacho. "Nothin'. Just pesterin' the prisoner so that he wouldn't get any rest while you were outside."

Dove gave him a hard stare. "He's my prisoner. I'll decide what to do with him."

"Sure," Graham murmured in reply to the rebuke. He went back to the wall and leaned against it.

Dove stood in front of the chair and lightly touched a fingertip to the gash on Nacho's cheek. So far, that was all she had done to his face, concentrating her efforts on his feet instead. Now she frowned in thought and said after a moment, "I think we'll move on to your hands next. Then the chest, and then your face. Unless you want to talk to me now."

He sat there, silent, his features stony.

"All right," she sighed, slipping the knife out of its sheath. "If that's what you want."

She must have cleaned the blade, Nacho thought. All the bloodstains were gone.

"Rider comin'!" one of the other men called from outside.

Dove whirled around, tensing. Livingston reached for his gun, and so did Graham. But then came another shout from the sentry. "It's your pa, Dove!"

"What does the old man want now?" she muttered, sliding the knife into its sheath.

"You'd better send him back to his cabin," Livingston told her. "I don't like the idea of our back trail being unprotected."

"Neither do I. Come on."

She stepped outside, accompanied by Livingston and Graham. Nacho could see them through the door that she left open behind her.

The three of them stopped and waited on the porch. Looking past them, Nacho caught a glimpse of a big, bearded man on horseback approaching the cabin. He recognized Seamus O'Shea. The old Comanchero rode right up to the porch before he reined in.

"What do you want?" Dove asked him sharply. "I told you to keep an eye on the trails and get rid of anybody who followed us."

"That's what I done," O'Shea grumbled, leaning forward in the saddle, shifting the Sharps he carried across the cantle and easing his old bones. "Figured you'd want t' know that lawyer fella an' Jake Maxwell showed up, lookin' for th' Meskin."

"You ran them off, didn't you?"

"Told 'em to go home. Had t' take a couple shots at 'em 'fore they got th' idea. But I reckon they'll be back, an' they'll bring a sheriff's posse with 'em next time." O'Shea took off his battered black hat and ran blunt fingers through his tangled hair. "Dove, I been thinkin'. You can't keep this up. From what Cambridge an' Maxwell said, they know th' preacher's mixed up in this, an' I reckon they even suspicion you are, too. It's time t' cut an' run, darlin'."

She glared at him and shook her head. "I don't run. Not anymore. I don't care what anyone knows about me."

"But if you stay, th' sheriff'll root you out sooner or later. Even ol' Massey ain't totally useless. But if you leave now, head for the high plains or the Panhandle, maybe, you got a chance t' get away clean. Just leave th' Meskin with me. You ain't killed him yet, have you?"

"He's alive," Dove said contemptuously. "But he won't be for long. What you just told me means there's no reason not to go ahead and kill him."

"I'm askin' you, Dove . . . don't do it."

She laughed. "Why the hell not?"

O'Shea's grip tightened on the Sharps as he brought the barrel around. "'Cause I'll stop you, girl."

She stared at him in amazement for a second, then laughed again and said, "Somebody kill this old fool."

Graham stepped forward, a savage grin on his face. "Be glad to, Dove," he said, and then his hand whipped toward the gun on his hip.

From the woods on the right side of the cabin, Jake Maxwell fired his Winchester.

The slug took Graham in the chest, driving him back against the wall of the cabin with a shocked look on his face. He hung there for an instant, his hand still reaching instinctively for his gun, then fell forward, dead before he crashed to the planks of the porch.

O'Shea twisted in the saddle, ignoring Dove and Livingston for the moment and going for one of the other outlaws who already had his gun out. The Sharps boomed. The heavy caliber bullet blew a fist-sized hole through the desperado and flung him backward. O'Shea kicked his feet free from the stirrups and tumbled out of the saddle.

Cambridge came in from the left, triggering his Colt. Two more outlaws dropped and the others who had been spread out in front of the cabin darted for cover. Livingston finally got his gun out as Cambridge reached the end of the porch. O'Shea had told the lawyer that Livingston wasn't very fast with a gun, and Cambridge saw now that was true. But the preacher managed to get a shot off as Dove ducked back inside.

The bullet whined past Cambridge's ear. Cambridge threw himself full-length on the porch and fired. Livingston staggered back a step, a bright red splash appearing on his white shirtfront. He groaned as he twisted sideways and collapsed.

Maxwell was still peppering the rest of the gang with rifle fire from the trees. Kneeling on one knee, O'Shea hauled out an ancient revolver and joined the exchange. Some of the outlaws tried to fight back, but others grabbed their horses and lit out. They were hardcases when the odds were overwhelmingly on their side, but they weren't willing to go up against the three grim-faced attackers.

Inside the cabin, Nacho had heard the sudden outbreak of gunfire and guessed that somehow Billy Cambridge had found him. He thought he recognized the sound of Jake Maxwell's Winchester, too. As Dove ran back inside, he caught a glimpse of Livingston shooting at something, then the phoney minister was jolted back out of Nacho's line of sight by a bullet.

Dove headed straight for him, the knife appearing in her hand as she came, and for an instant, Nacho thought she was going to drive the blade into his heart. But then she went past him, crouching behind the chair and putting the razor-sharp edge to his throat.

Seamus O'Shea appeared in the doorway, with Cambridge at his side. "Back away from him, Dove," O'Shea ordered.

She was pressed so close against the chair that Nacho could feel the shake of her head. "You back away," she said. "Let me ride clear or I'll slit his throat."

O'Shea looked over at Cambridge. Sweat trickled down Nacho's brow and into his eyes, even though it wasn't hot at all today. A muscle twitched in Cambridge's cheek, and then he said, "She can go. Nacho's life is worth more to me than hers."

"You heard th' man, Dove," O'Shea said. "Let him go."

"Get out of here first, all of you. I want everyone to ride away. Then you can have him back."

Nacho met Cambridge's eyes and somehow conveyed the message to go along with her. She had proven over and over that she couldn't be trusted, but they had no choice now.

"You'll be all right, Nacho," Cambridge said, trying to sound reassuring.

"Sure, Billy." Nacho forced some of his former jauntiness into his voice. "I'll be fine."

Cambridge and O'Shea backed up, but before they got out of sight, the lawyer called out, "All the rest of the gang took off for the tall and uncut, Dove, the ones that still could. You'll be leaving alone."

"Get the hell out of here!" she cried in response, and Nacho could tell from the quiver in her voice that she was walking a fine line now.

Cambridge and O'Shea disappeared, but a few minutes later they rode into sight again, this time accompanied by Jake Maxwell. Turning so that Dove could still see them from the cabin, they rode away, not looking back.

Dove took the knife away from Nacho's throat, and a second later, he felt it slice through the cords holding him to the chair. "Stand up," she said.

He sagged forward, fighting off the pain and weariness that were trying to claim him. "I . . . I don't know if I can walk."

"You'd damn well better be able to, if you want to live a little while longer. You're coming with me."

Nacho put his hands on his knees and forced himself up. While he was doing that, Dove pried up a loose board from the floor and took out a large canvas bag that appeared to be stuffed full. She slung it over her shoulder by a rawhide strap that was attached to it. The loot from the gang's hold-ups, Nacho thought. He staggered toward the doorway, biting his lip against the agony every time his lacerated feet came down on the rough planks of the floor. The point of Dove's knife pricked the middle of his back, right above his heart, and stayed there.

When they reached the porch, Dove said, "Wait a minute." He glanced back over his shoulder and saw her looking at the sprawled body of John Livingston. There was no remorse, no grief on her face, only the faintest hint of a smile.

Those soldiers back at Fort Griffin had been responsible for more than the death of Dove's mother, Nacho realized. The girl's soul had died that day, too.

She stepped away from him but didn't give him a chance to try to escape. Scooping up Livingston's fallen six-gun, she trained the barrel on him and said, "Keep going. Grab a couple of those horses."

Several saddled horses were milling around in front of the cabin, no doubt belonging to the handful of outlaws who had been killed in the attack. Nacho saw the bodies lying here and there around the outside of the cabin, including Graham's. He felt sick at the the sight and stepped down from the porch, calling softly to the nervous animals. In a matter of minutes, he had the reins of two of them.

"Mount up," Dove said, taking one of the horses from him. He put a bare foot in the stirrup, gripped the saddlehorn tightly, and clenched his teeth. It hurt like hell as he swung up into the saddle.

Dove was ready to go. She took the canvas bag from her shoulder and hung it from the horn. With her other hand, she kept the gun pointed in Nacho's general direction. She glanced back at the cabin and said, "It wasn't a bad hide-out. I'll miss it. But there'll be another one."

"And . . . and another gang?" Nacho asked. Out of the corner of his eye, he looked around for any sign of Cambridge and the others, certain that they hadn't deserted him.

"Of course. There's plenty more like Graham. The West is full of them."

"What about Livingston?"

"I'm not going to waste any tears over him, if that's what you mean. He said he loved me, but he didn't mean it. He'd have left someday . . . just like my mother left. Just like my father . . ." She spat on the ground. "People who say they love you always leave."

"Dove . . . when I first saw you . . . I loved you, too."

Her features twisted with hate and he knew he shouldn't have said it. As she brought the gun up and eared back the hammer, she said, "Well, that's just too damned bad for you."

The slug drove her out of the saddle, spinning her to the ground. She didn't even cry out as she died.

Nacho looked toward the sound of the shot. It had come from a rise a good three hundred yards away. A hell of a shot. A shot that Billy Cambridge couldn't have made on his best day, and Nacho had a feeling Jake Maxwell couldn't have, either.

That only left one man—Seamus O'Shea.

Nacho reached out and lifted the bag of stolen money from Dove's horse. He didn't look at her as he turned his own mount and urged it into motion, riding out to meet the other men.

It was a long way and he hurt, but he felt pretty sure he could make it.